Sammy's Story
Book 17 in Culpepper Cowboys
Kirsten Osbourne

Chapter 1

Samantha Ross locked the door of her clinic to head into Culpepper, Wyoming. She had heard there was a new bookstore in town, and she was willing to forgo her daily burger at Bob's Burger Barn to go there and see what she could see. She wasn't expecting anything along the lines of a Barnes and Noble, of course, because it was in a small town, but hopefully, it would at least have a nice little romance section. She couldn't express how excited she was at the idea of holding real books she'd never read in her hands again and not just her Kindle.

She was halfway there when she realized she had to have lunch anyway. Thankfully the burger barn and the new bookstore were side by side.

She parked in the burger barn parking lot, and then rushed inside. Bob was there, looking grumpy as usual, and she hurried to him. "Can I get my usual but to go?"

Bob nodded, writing down her order. "Sure. Megan's supposed to see you this week, right?"

Sammy nodded. "Yeah. I can't believe you two are expecting again already." She grinned at him. Sammy was the local midwife in Culpepper, and her older sister, Tabby, was the OB/GYN. They often helped each other out.

"I can't either. Of course, I wasn't expecting little Bethany, so what do I know about anything?" Bob couldn't help but grin when he mentioned his little girl, transforming his usually grumpy face.

Sammy grinned. "It'll be nice that they're so close together. They'll be friends!"

"I sure hope so." Bob shook his head. "Having to be the best friend of an eighteen-month-old girl is hard. I spend more time burping baby dolls than I do making burgers!"

"Sounds about right!" She glanced at the time on her phone. "I'll be back in about thirty for the burger. I have a real ache in me to check out the bookstore next door. I'm so excited that Culpepper finally has a bookstore!"

"Enjoy yourself. Your food will be ready."

Sammy handed him a ten, knowing the food would cost around seven. "Keep the change." With those words, she hurried out the door. She had to see what books were there.

The sign above the bookstore read, "Barry's Books." She grinned, taking a deep breath before pushing open the door. She knew in a moment she would be assailed with the scent of books—real books—and she couldn't wait.

She pushed the door open and stood just inside for a moment, filling her senses with the look, feel, and smell of a bookstore. "Whoever Barry is, I already love him," she mumbled softly enough for her ears only.

From right beside her, she heard, "You do, do you?" The voice was deep and masculine and scared her half out of her mind.

Sammy jumped, her hand going to her chest. "Where'd you come from? You scared me!"

"I was working on a display right there," he said, pointing to a spot right behind her, right next to the front door of the shop. "I'm Barry Hamilton, by the way. Since you love me now, you should know that I'm the one you love."

"So nice to meet you, Barry. I'm Sammy Ross." She tried to hide her embarrassment at him hearing her, but she knew that her blush hid nothing.

"Nice to meet you, Sammy Ross. What kind of book can I interest you in?" he asked. "I have new and used in just about every genre imaginable." He rubbed his hands together, obviously excited to help a customer.

Sammy's face lit up at the prospect of all the books she could look through. "Romance. I want all the romance you've got."

Barry grinned. "Well, Valentine's Day is tomorrow. I'll pick you up at seven, and I'll show you *real* romance."

She laughed softly. "I think you know I meant romance books, but I'm going to take you up on that date now, and you're going to run for the hills." He was incredibly handsome, and she was ready to spend some time with him.

"Have you looked in a mirror in the past ten years? No man is going to run for the hills at the idea of dating you." He pulled his phone from his pocket. "Sammy Ross. Address and phone number please."

She immediately recited her address and phone number, wondering what was going on with this man. "Now, books!"

He laughed. "You came here for books and not for me?"

"I didn't know you, but I'm intimately acquainted with books."

"Intimately, huh? I wouldn't mind being intimately acquainted with you!"

She blushed again, shaking her head. "I'll just wander around then, shall I?"

"I couldn't make you do that. Let me show you to the romance section, small though it is. I'm sorry to say, I'm not much of a connoisseur of romance novels, so I never know what to get."

"You need a female partner to help you with these things."

"Are you looking for a job?" he asked, winking at her.

"No, I'm a little too busy for that. I'm the local midwife."

His head tilted to one side. "Midwifery? Really?"

"Yes. Really. My sister is an OB/GYN. We share a clinic and work together a lot. If I get a complicated case, they see her."

"Interesting." He led her to the romance section and waved at it. "Here's my ridiculously small romance section. If you'd just give me a list of your favorite authors while we're out tomorrow night, I'll make sure I carry them."

Sammy grinned at him. "You don't really have to take me out tomorrow night. I'm sure you have better things to do for Valentine's

Day." The man was . . . well, sexy didn't begin to cut it. His muscles seemed to have muscles. Her fingers ached to touch him.

"I don't. I just moved to Culpepper three weeks ago. I don't know anyone, so you're it. You're not going to back out and leave me all alone for my first holiday in town, are you?"

She laughed. "No, I won't. And I want to talk to you all day, but I need a book first, so go away, and I'll see you tomorrow night."

Barry looked at her for a moment before laughing aloud. "You're something else, Sammy Ross."

She winked at him and turned away, her entire mind on romances now. How much of her lunch hour had she spent flirting? Way too much, she was afraid!

She dug through the books, and twenty minutes later, she was at the cash register with ten different books. She gave him her debit card to ring them up. "Thank you so much. I'm so glad we finally have a bookstore in town, but I have to say, your romance section is more than a little pathetic. I'll help you with that."

"It can't be too bad if you found ten books."

"I'm a voracious reader. What can I say?" She took the bag of books and waved at him. "See you tomorrow night."

Barry stood watching the front door of the shop, smiling. Sammy Ross was something a lot more special than she or anyone in this town could possibly realize. He was going to keep her. Whether she knew it and liked it or not.

* * *

Sammy was still thinking about Barry when she got back to the clinic for her next appointment. One of her favorite writers, Jolene Gold, was expecting her second child, and she had decided to go the midwife route this time. Sammy put her taco burger and fried cheese curds in the microwave to keep them warm while she examined Jolene—whose real name was May.

At the end of Jolene's appointment, Sammy smiled. "You're doing great. Just keep doing everything you've been doing. Are you taking your prenatal vitamins every day?"

"Except when they make me throw up."

Sammy frowned. "Are you still throwing up a lot? You're in the middle of your second trimester."

"I did the same thing when I was pregnant with Bobbette. I do the all-day sickness for nine months thing. I think this is going to have to be our last child, because I can't keep doing this."

"And here I was going to ask you when your next book would be out . . ."

Jolene laughed. "Well, since I have a full-time nanny, I would say the middle of next week."

"You're a superhero, writing through your morning sickness this way." Sammy smiled. "I can talk to Tabby about getting you something for the nausea."

"I never took anything last time. I'm not sure I want any drugs in my system while I'm pregnant." Jolene shrugged. "What would you do if you were pregnant?"

"Well, as a midwife, I don't like any drugs at all during pregnancy. I probably wouldn't take anything if you have the ability to power through. I know how many books you write, though, and I don't want you to get stressed about falling behind."

Jolene sighed. "I think I can power through. I will be announcing the pregnancy on my social media soon, and then everyone will just tell me to do what I can. My fans are amazing."

"All right. I'll see you in a month, then. You let me know if you change your mind, and Tabby will see you."

"I don't think I'm going to, but thanks." Jolene reached into her purse and pulled out a book. "I thought you might like this."

Sammy's eyes grew wide. *"Sammy's Story?* It's about me?"

Jolene nodded. "Sure is. I dedicated it to you as well."

Sammy threw her arms around her patient and favorite author. "You're the best! Have I told you yet how much I love you?"

"I'll see you next month." Jolene left with a grin on her face, and Sammy flipped to the dedication. "For Samantha Ross: Thank you for always taking such good care of me. You're the best midwife a romance writer could ask for."

Sammy sniffed as she walked back to the microwave for her lunch. She had fifteen minutes until her next patient arrived. She opened the book and started reading, doing her best not to get any of her taco burger on it.

* * *

Just before it was time for her to close for the day, her sister popped her head in from her clinic. "How'd everything go? Need me for anything?"

Sammy shook her head. "Not really. I mean, I might need you to take a look at May Bodefeld," she said, carefully remembering the woman's real name. "She's got all-day sickness and is halfway through her second trimester. Other than that, everything is pretty routine."

"She probably needs some meds, if she'll take them." Tabby came all the way into the clinic, and Sammy smiled at her sister's huge belly. She was due soon, and Sammy would have the privilege of delivering the baby.

"She told me she doesn't want to take anything and she's going to try to power through. I know she's working all the time and not giving herself a rest at all, though, so I think she might eventually need you." Sammy patted her examining table, and Tabby laboriously climbed up. "How are you feeling?"

Tabby shrugged. "I'm not feeling anything unusual. Just ready for the baby to come, and I am doing all the normal nesting stuff."

"Are you looking forward to your shower on Saturday?" Sammy asked, her hands going to her sister's stomach.

"Absolutely! I'm so excited. I'm glad we decided on just a female shower. Arch and his buddies are going to go off and do something manly. Don't ask me what, because it sounded tiresome to me."

Sammy grinned. "I think they're going to Austin's bar for a dart tournament. Kolby asked Austin to do it, and you know how tight those two are. So they're setting up prizes and an entry fee and everything. They can have their fun, while we have ours."

"Sounds good to me. Who made the cake?"

"Who do you think?"

"Grace Wells. Is she doing one of her famous belly cakes?"

"Yup. She was sure that would fit you nicely." Sammy didn't mention that the belly would have a stethoscope on it, because she wanted Tabby to be at least a little surprised.

"How is her little boy doing? Are she and Marcus still happy?"

"Oh, yeah! I watched baby Joe the other night. He's so much fun!"

"You need to get married and have babies of your own, Sam. I worry about you always being alone." Tabby was wearing her big sister face, but Sammy just shook her head.

"Are you going to arrange for me to marry? Like I did for you?" Sammy referred to the wedding she'd tricked her sister into.

"No, I wouldn't be so presumptuous. But you haven't dated in forever!" Tabby frowned at Sammy. "You've never really dated, have you?"

"I have a date tomorrow night," Sammy said softly. "Barry, the guy who owns the new bookstore next to Bob's Burger Barn."

"Really? Is he taking you dancing?"

"I sure hope so!" Sammy grinned. "I don't know what we're doing, but he's picking me up at seven. Are you done worrying about me?"

Tabby frowned. "I think I might have to have Arch check him out."

"Arch is not my keeper, and neither are you. Get a grip and let me live my life!" Sammy knew her words were harsh, but Tabby had been on her to find a boyfriend and marry since she'd gotten married a little over two years ago. She needed to back off and let Sammy live her own life.

"Fine. I'm not going to say anything else about it."

Tabby didn't look offended, but she looked like she was scheming. *God help me.* "I mean it, Tab. I don't want anyone interfering. I like him, but that doesn't mean we're meant to be together. It just means he owns a bookstore, and I want at his goods."

"As long as you mean the goods in his store and not the goods in his pants . . ."

Sammy rolled her eyes. "Go away."

"Hey, I'm your favorite sister!" Tabby protested.

"Right now, you're my *least* favorite sister!"

"Only sister!"

Sammy shook her head. "I have new books to read. Go home and play with Arch, and I'll read my books."

"I'm going! I'm going!" Tabby carefully got down off the table and hugged Sammy. "Love you."

"Love you back." Sammy watched her sister go with a smile, and then she went into the little home attached to the back of the clinic she shared with her sister. She opened the crock pot and served herself some of the chili she'd put in there before work that morning and sat down at the table, book in hand. She was going to read and read and read, and nothing made her happier.

* * *

Sammy was sitting in her regular booth at Bob's Burger Barn the next day at lunch, a book in hand. She was waiting on her taco burger as she read and not paying attention to anything around her.

"Is this seat taken?" asked a masculine voice, and she looked up.

"Hey, Barry. Have a seat." She was surprised to see him there, but she wasn't sure why. He did work at the next building over, after all.

"Do you eat lunch here every day?" he asked.

"I do. I love the taco burger. I remember when he was working on it, and as soon as it came onto the menu, I got it. I've had it just about every day since, because it's *amazing.*"

"I haven't tried it yet. Maybe I'll get that today."

"I always get the taco burger and a side of fried cheese curds. Then I feel sick as I go back to work, but it's so amazing, I just can't seem to stop." Sammy knew she shouldn't divulge secrets about her terrible eating habits with a man she wanted to date, but she couldn't seem to help herself.

He looked at the book in her hand. "Did you get that from me yesterday?"

She nodded excitedly. "Yup. One of my favorite authors, and I hadn't read this one yet. I only buy hers in paperback because I want to be able to keep them."

"That makes sense." He tilted his head to one side. "What is it you like about that author so much?"

"I love the marriage of convenience stories."

Barry shook his head. "You've lost me. What's marriage of convenience?"

"It's when two people marry for reasons other than love. Like if they marry because his wife died and left him with triplets. Or if he needs to be married for an inheritance, so he marries her, and they eventually fall in love. Those are my favorites."

"Really? I'm not sure I understand the appeal of that, but I'm not a woman, so that may be why."

"What did you do before opening a bookstore? And how did you end up in Culpepper?"

"I've been through the area for rodeos many times. I used to ride broncs. When I was thrown and broke my leg in a way that will never totally heal, I decided it was time to stop riding, and I figured I'd open a bookstore. The other guys on the rodeo circuit used to make fun of me for reading so much, but I've always loved books." He shrugged. "I miss the rodeo at times, but I like the idea of building a business of my own and not destroying my body in the process."

"Have you ever thought about writing, or do you just read?"

He seemed embarrassed for a moment, and Bob came by then to slide Sammy's food in front of her. "There you go." He looked at Barry. "What are you hungry for?"

Barry looked at Sammy's taco burger. "I think I want to try the taco burger and a side of fried cheese curds."

"You're corrupting the man," Bob said to Sammy before wandering off.

"Well? Have you thought about writing?" she asked again.

He nodded. "I'm actually working on writing a book between customers and shelving books and other store duties. It's a sci-fi story set in 2346, and I'm really excited about it."

"You'll have to let me read what you've written so far! Is there romance in it?"

He shook his head. "Not in sci-fi!"

"There's no point in writing a book with no romance. Trust me, you need romance. Add some!"

He just laughed, snagging one of her cheese curds. "We'll see."

Chapter 2

Getting ready for her date that night was a struggle for Sammy. She had no idea what they were doing, so knowing what to wear was virtually impossible. She decided that dressing in western wear might be the best bet, given his history. She put on a pair of jeans, a button up shirt, and a pair of green cowgirl boots. She decided not to go nuts and top it off with her favorite hat, because that would seem like overkill.

When Barry came to the door—exactly at seven—she smiled to see he'd worn very close to the same thing. "Hi!"

Barry grinned. "Hi. You ready? Weather doesn't look great, but I think we're all right if we stick around Culpepper." Truthfully, only an idiot would get out in the weather they were having if they didn't need to, but for her, he'd be an idiot all day.

"Sounds good to me. What are we eating?" He'd treated her to Bob's for lunch, so she wasn't sure what else he had up his sleeve.

"I was thinking we could stop at the diner for supper and then go to the bar for some dancing."

Sammy bit her lip. She wasn't a drinker and preferred not to be in the company of someone who drank—especially if they were driving. "I'm not really fond of alcohol." She'd lost a friend to a drunk driving accident when she'd been in college for her RN, and she hated the idea of being around anyone drunk as a result.

"I don't drink at all. I saw too many accidents that were caused by alcohol when I was on the road. I just want to dance."

"But you won't drink?" Sammy asked. She had to be certain. It was the line she'd drawn for herself—not drinking or dating anyone who drank—and she refused to lie to herself.

"I won't drink at all. Unless you consider a root beer a drink."

"I don't." She grinned at him, happy they were seeing eye to eye on the subject. She hopped into the passenger side of his truck and quickly buckled up. "I like your truck."

"Thanks. You like the snow plow on the front? I put that there just for our date." He knew there was a good chance they'd be stuck somewhere, and if he could alleviate the hassle of it with a plow on the front, he sure would.

"Oh, it's lovely. Best thing I've ever seen!" And it was, because it meant they could get home, no matter how much snow fell that night.

He grinned. "I don't like to have to close my shop on snow days, so I made it so I can handle whatever snow falls all on my own."

"Very smart of you."

"I think so." He grinned at her, noting she was watching him drive. "So what kind of schooling is involved in becoming a midwife?"

"Well, I'm a CNM, certified nurse midwife. I did four years of college to become an RN, and then I did one year of nursing. Then another three years to get my masters in nursing with a concentration in midwifery. My sister and I really had the same goal, but we went about it in different ways. But we rely on each other when we need to."

"So if you're delivering a baby and there's a complication, she helps out?"

"Yes! She's done c-sections on my patients when medically necessary, and I assist in almost all her births. We work together a lot more than you'd think. Most midwives don't have a doctor they work so closely with, but this works well for both of us."

Barry had never thought about a practice like that. "So if you get pregnant, does your sister deliver the baby?"

Sammy laughed softly. "Well, since Tabby is due in a few weeks, and I'm delivering *her* baby, I would think so."

"Really?" He shook his head. "Interesting." He parked the car in the parking lot of the diner, looking over at her. "I'm glad you agreed to come out with me tonight."

"Me too." She grinned at him. "And not just because you love books like I do."

"Well, the book thing has to be the draw. I should have realized I should have a bigger romance section when I designed the layout for the store. The more romance, the more women, I would think."

"That makes a lot of sense," she said with a grin. "Make it happen!"

He laughed softly. "I'll need your help to design it."

"Happy to do it! And we'll design it right. There'll be a section for time-travel romance. Another for marriage of convenience. Yet another for billionaire. And another for secret babies. Another for shifters. You'll have the best romance bookstore in the whole country!"

"Umm . . . is there still room for science fiction? I do *love* my science fiction."

She sighed. "I guess we can leave a tiny corner of the store open for sci-fi."

He shook his head, opening his door and getting out. He hurried around to help her down. "Careful. It's slick over here."

"You must have seen me try to walk on ice before. I will do my best not to break myself on our date."

"That's a relief!" he said with a grin.

They stomped the snow from their feet as they entered the diner.

"Two of you?" the hostess asked.

"How are you doing, Maggie?" Sammy asked after Barry nodded in answer to Maggie's question.

"Tired! I hope you didn't get your feelings hurt when I went to Tabby this time. After that emergency c-section last time, I just felt better starting out with an OB/GYN." Maggie looked at her as if she was nervous of her answer.

"Don't even worry about it, Maggie. I'll still be there for the birth, and you'll be in great hands with my sister. All is good as long as your baby is born healthy."

Maggie smiled. "I'm so glad you see it that way. John and I debated and debated, but in the end, we want to have Tabby ready to take the baby."

"I understand that perfectly. My sister is always on call when I deliver for a reason." Sammy slid into the booth.

"Drinks?" Maggie asked, looking back and forth between them.

"I want a Sprite."

"Root beer," Barry said.

As she walked away, Barry smiled. "You really did handle that well. I hope you know that."

"I did my best. I feel like having the best medical help you can when you deliver a baby is the right thing to do."

"I'm not going to ask a lot of questions about your work, because I really don't want to know a lot about the birthing process. I've helped cows and horses but never humans."

"Where did you grow up?" she asked.

He shrugged. "Kind of all over. My parents divorced when I was young, and my mother remarried. A lot. It was kind of like the show Gypsy. There's a song in there where they talk about their mother getting married. And married. And married. That's what my life was like. Mom would remarry, and then I'd go to another state. I spent my high school years in western Wyoming, and I learned my love of bull riding there. But I've lived in New York City, Texas, California, and Idaho. Pretty much all over."

"Are you an only child?" she asked.

He shook his head. "No, I have a half-brother who is five years younger than me. I keep trying to get him to move here and help me run my bookstore."

"What does he do?"

"He's a bull-rider. He went on the rodeo circuit just like I did. I hope he retires soon." It was strange how much he worried about his brother when he was just doing the same thing he'd done.

"What's his name?"

"Bart. My mother thought she was cute, naming us Barry and Bart. She's a mess."

"Where is she now?"

He shrugged. "California again was the last I heard. The longest she ever stayed anywhere was while I was in high school. I don't miss that lifestyle."

"But it sounds like you kind of went into it when you were on the circuit. Am I misunderstanding?"

He looked shocked for a moment. "I never really thought of that!" He'd chosen as his first job something that would make him continue the way of life he'd hated growing up.

"People tend to return to the things that make them most comfortable. You are used to never knowing anyone for long and moving on. So that's what you do." She hoped he was there to stay.

"I thought you were a midwife, not a psychologist."

She grinned. "There was a waiting list for nursing school, so I have a dual degree in nursing and psychology. Fun, huh?"

Barry made a face. "I'm not so sure about that one!"

She giggled. "Well, I like it!"

"So tell me about the area. What do you like to do in the winter?"

Sammy thought about it for a moment. "I love snowmobiling. I would spend every waking hour doing that. Well, if I could divide snowmobiling and reading by the fire, that would be good. I like to sled as well. I just kind of like winter, I guess. Except shoveling snow. We have a four-wheeler with a plow on the front for the clinic parking lot, but it's not as much fun as it sounds."

He laughed. "I have been plowing my parking lot with my truck. Hopefully people will start coming in."

"Business is slow?" she asked, concerned.

"A little. I've been told the spring and summer will bring in more people and they will buy books. We'll see. I won't give up, and going between customers gives me time to write."

"That's right! Tell me about your book!"

He shook his head. "I'm superstitious. I don't want to talk about it until it's completely done and edited. Then I'll probably be begging you to read it and give me your opinion on it."

"I'm happy to do that. I love the idea of having a writer for a . . . friend." She'd started to say boyfriend but thought better of it. They'd only known one another for a day and a half. Calling him a boyfriend this soon just might mess with his head.

"Well, you've got one." He grinned. "So you seem to always be around babies with your career. Do you want kids?"

She smiled tentatively. "I want dozens of kids. Seriously. I'd have as many as I could. Of course, I'm thirty-three, and I need to start soon if I'm going to have any of them at all."

He frowned at that. "You need to find a man to marry quick then. Maybe I should hide under the table." What he felt like doing was standing and saying he volunteered as tribute. He wasn't sure how that would make her react, though.

She laughed. "I promise, I'm not going to dig my claws into you and never let you go. I need to get to know a man before I see him as the father of my future imaginary children."

"That's probably good news for me." He leaned back as Maggie brought their drinks. "Do you know what you want?"

Maggie laughed. "Even I know what she wants. This one is a creature of habit. She's having the Salisbury steak with mashed potatoes and brown gravy." She turned her attention to Barry. "You?"

He shrugged. "That sounds good to me."

"You don't have to get it just because I am. Take some time to look if you want." Sammy felt like she'd forced him to eat what she liked for lunch. She didn't want to do the same thing for supper.

"No, it really sounds good."

Maggie nodded and hurried away.

"So . . . I got you a Valentine's gift . . ." he said.

"How did you do that so quick? I didn't get anything for you!" Sammy suddenly felt like a heel.

Barry grinned. "Then I get to kiss you goodnight for my gift."

She frowned. "It sounds like you've thought this out a little too far . . ."

"Maybe I have." He reached over and covered her hand with his. "I think I already like you a lot. I want to know if there's a chance it'll go anywhere, and a goodnight kiss will tell me." If they had half the chemistry between them he thought they did, then it was going to be fabulous.

"I guess it will." Sammy was only worried about kissing him because she was so attracted to him. She was afraid she'd melt into a puddle in his arms, and she had to work the next day.

He pulled something from under the table, and she wondered how he'd gotten it there. She hadn't seen him carry anything in from the car.

"What is it?" she asked, frowning.

"It's your gift." It was wrapped nicely with heart-covered wrapping paper.

"Did you wrap this yourself?" she asked. She'd always been terrible at wrapping gifts, and admired anyone who could do a good job.

"No way! I had the company I ordered it from wrap it."

"How did you get it so quick?"

Barry frowned at her. "Some secrets shall never be revealed!"

Sammy shook her head, loving his lighthearted sense of humor. The man was growing on her—like a fungus. She carefully opened the gift and pulled out a box of chocolate. Turning over the heart shaped box, she found the name of the company. "Frank's Fudge? You got me Frank's Fudge? And this is why I knew before I ever saw you that I'd fall in love with you. Frank's Fudge is my favorite *ever!*"

Barry grinned. "I hoped you'd like it!"

"Did you get the Erin? Those are my absolute favorites. Milk chocolate, caramel, and sea salt. I can already taste them!"

He nodded. "I did get the Erin. You seem to know Frank's Fudge well."

"What you probably don't know yet, because you're new to town, is that Megan, Bob's wife from Bob's Burger Barn, has a sister who married Al Frank, the owner of Frank's Fudge. Those of us who didn't know the company before that sure know it now. We want to support Al and Erin, because we love Megan and Bob!"

"You're right. I didn't know that. But I love that you do." Barry would be constantly surprised by the people of this town and how much they knew about one another.

Sammy hugged the heart-shaped box to her chest, and then stuffed it in her purse. "You're definitely getting that good night kiss."

Barry grinned. "Only if you *want* to kiss me. I was kidding about that being your return gift for me. I'm glad you like the chocolate, though. I met Al a few years back, and once I'd tried his fudge, I knew I was going to eat only his chocolate forever."

"You have awfully good taste in chocolate, then."

Maggie brought their food then, sliding a plate in front of each of them. "If you need anything else, just yell."

"Thanks, Maggie. Go put your feet up!"

"Don't think I won't!" Maggie hurried off toward the kitchen, making Sammy glad the diner wasn't very busy.

"I guess the weather kept most people at home tonight. Good. We have the whole place to ourselves. Maybe the bar will be the same." Sammy looked at her supper and grinned. It was definitely her favorite thing the diner served.

"Have you met the guy who runs it? Austin?"

"Yeah, Austin is amazing. I love his wife, Dallas. I delivered her baby, come to think of it."

"Wait . . . Austin married Dallas? Two Texas cities?"

Sammy nodded emphatically. "Yup. Craziness, huh? They were meant for each other before either of them even knew it."

"That's really cool, actually." He took a bite of his supper and smiled. "You choose food well. The next time we go out, you're going to just have to tell me what I'm getting."

"Oh? Are we going out again?"

"Well, unless you're a terrible kisser. If you slobber all over me, then I'll have to dump you." Barry stabbed his fork into his Salisbury steak to punctuate what he was saying.

She laughed. "I see where your priorities are!"

"Do you have plans for the weekend?" he asked. Really, he wanted to know if she was seeing anyone else, but he didn't want to come right out and ask.

"Yeah, I'm throwing a baby shower for my sister. Should be fun. All the men are going to the bar and having a dart tournament. You should join them!"

"When is this shower?" he asked, hating that she was going to be too busy to see him.

"We're doing it Saturday evening. From six to eight." Sammy shrugged. "It seemed like it was the best time for everyone."

"All right. So you're free Friday night and Sunday night?"

She nodded. "Mostly. I do church on Sunday morning. Have you been to the church in town? Brother Anthony's weddings are . . . phenomenal. And I have to decorate for the shower tomorrow night. We're doing it at the clinic, and it's going to be a lot of work." She wished she'd had the foresight to ask some of the women in town to help decorate, but she was on her own.

"How can a wedding be phenomenal? They're all the same."

"Not Brother Anthony's! Seriously, if you get invited to a wedding he's presiding over, you have to go. It's crazy how good they are."

"I'll keep that in mind. I don't seem to be at the top of anyone's wedding invitation list yet, but give me time!"

They kept talking while they ate, discussing all the different people in town. "Have you been to the bakery yet?" Sammy asked. "I like to go every morning for the kolaches. I either run over there in the mornings to get them, or I have to do thirty minutes on my treadmill every night. The food is fattening, but *so* good!"

"I haven't. Is it here in town?" He was a fan of kolaches because of the time he'd spent in Texas.

"Actually no. It's off the Culpepper ranch."

"Ahh . . . that's why I haven't seen it. I've met the three Culpepper brothers, though."

"There are four!" Sammy said. "Karlan, Cooper, Kolby, and Chris."

"Oh, hmm . . . I think I've met Karlan, Cooper, and Kolby."

"Chris is married to Chastity."

"Why are there so many names like that around town? I mean the virtuous names. I've never seen anything like it."

"Wow. You don't know much about the town, do you?"

He shook his head. "Not really. What am I missing?" He knew she would know everything there was to know, but he didn't want to seem too terribly nosy. Now he had to know!

Sammy blinked. "A lot. Let me tell you about Culpepper, Wyoming. About four years ago, there was this photoshoot on a ranch near town. It was for male underwear models. When word got out that there were hunky male models on a ranch near town, all the women in town rushed out there on different pretenses. Even a lot of the married women, if I'm totally honest with you. And then there was a blizzard. . . . So many women were trapped there with the models. So then there were pregnancies and weddings following it. There weren't many women left in Culpepper after that . . ."

He frowned at her. "You're kidding, right?"

"Not at all. Well then, the Culpeppers' grandfather died. And he stipulated in the will that all four brothers had to be married within a month of the reading of the will, and at least one brother had to have a baby on the way by the end of the year. Or their ridiculous cousin who cared nothing about ranches would inherit."

"With no women left? Well, you were here . . ."

"Yeah, but no one was interested in me. Everyone knew Tabby would end up with Arch, so she was kind of forbidden, and we were always linked as sisters, so I was ignored, as if I was supposed to be with Arch, too. It was weird."

"So where did they get wives from?"

"Well, they contacted a matchmaker, who sent out quadruplets, and let each of the brothers choose. Those quadruplets were Hope, Faith, Joy, and Chastity Quinlan. Each of them married one of the Culpepper brothers. Then their younger sisters, twins of course, joined them. Grace and Honor came with their cousins, Patience and Felicity. So we had eight Quinlans with names like that. See?"

"I see it's all confusing and giving me a headache."

She laughed. "We all feel that way at times."

Chapter 3

After supper, Barry and Sammy went straight to Austin's bar, the Culpepper Watering Hole. When they arrived, they realized the weather really had kept most people away. There was only one couple on the dance floor, and they were Austin and his wife, Dallas. There was a live band in the corner, and the bands usually brought in a crowd.

Austin smiled at them, kissing his wife's cheek and heading toward them. "Do you need anything from the bar?"

"Soft drinks maybe?" Barry looked at Sammy. "Thirsty?"

"No, but I will be after a couple of dances. Sprite?"

"You want me to make it a Shirley Temple? That's what Dallas and I drink."

Sammy grinned. "Sounds wonderful!"

Barry walked off to the bar with Austin. Sammy headed straight for Dallas. "Who's babysitting tonight?"

Dallas grinned. "The best thing about teaching high school is that I always know who isn't dating and is available to babysit for date night. Tonight, it's Alisha Waters. She broke up with her boyfriend last week, and she's my favorite babysitter anyway. She's wonderful."

"I've heard about her babysitting. She's supposed to be great with kids."

"Oh, she is. I hate that she's sad after breaking up with scumbag Michael, but he was using her to do his homework anyway. I know the type." Dallas shook her head. "She's better off making a few bucks and playing with a baby."

"Very true." Sammy smiled. "You guys planning another? I wouldn't mind delivering."

Dallas laughed. "You know we'll come straight to you if we end up pregnant again. And yes, we'd like one more. We were both lonely onlies, and we'd like to spare our child that."

"I can understand that completely."

Austin and Barry returned with the drinks, and they put them on an empty table. Barry took Sammy's hand in his. "May I have this dance?"

Sammy laughed. "For tonight, you get *every* dance."

"I'd prefer forever, but I'll take tonight." Barry winked at her.

She shook her head, moving into his arms to the slow song the band was playing. "I hope they do slow songs all night." She loved to dance, but she didn't feel comfortable with fast songs. Slow songs were what made her happy.

"Austin told me he requested only slow songs. He prefers to dance to the slow ones, too, and he's enjoying a nice night with his wife. His bartender called in afraid to drive through the snow, but with it only being them and us, he's fine with it."

Sammy was surprised at just how good his arms felt around her. She rested her head on his shoulder, letting herself think of possibilities with this man for the first time since she'd met him. Until that moment, he was just someone to have fun with for one night. Now . . . well, maybe there *could* be a future between them.

Barry's hands stroked her back gently as they slow danced together. He couldn't believe just how good she felt in his arms. When he'd first seen her and she'd claimed to be in love with him, he had been more attracted than he'd ever been, but he'd expected the feelings to subside when he touched her. Nothing could feel that strong, could it? Apparently, he was wrong.

They danced four dances together before the band announced they were taking a break until the next set. While they took their break, the four of them sat at a table together.

Dallas looked at Barry. "I don't think I know you. Do you live in Culpepper?" She took a sip of her Shirley Temple.

"I opened the new bookstore, Barry's Books. It's next to Bob's Burger Barn."

Dallas smiled. "I love books! I hope you have a good romance section."

Barry looked back and forth between Dallas and Sammy. "I hope you two are best friends, because you've said the exact same thing to me."

Sammy smiled. "We're friendly. I delivered their baby eighteen months ago, and she's adorable."

"I didn't realize you were a romance novel fan," Dallas said, looking at Sammy. "Maybe I *do* need a new best friend . . ."

Austin shrugged. "I'll stop being your best friend if I can stay your husband. Either way is good for me."

Barry laughed. "I guess being best friends with your spouse would be the best possible scenario."

"It is." Dallas looked over at Austin with a soft smile on her face. "But he's been my best friend since third grade."

Austin took her hand in his. "Back then I told everyone who would listen that I was going to run away with her and marry her, and we were going to live under the monkey bars, and I would fish to feed us." He shook his head. "I'd still live under monkey bars with you any day."

Dallas laughed. "If only you'd been able to convince me of how you felt sooner."

"It wasn't my fault you were stubborn and unbending!"

Sammy grinned at the play between the married couple. "I always wondered why you two married so quickly as soon as you moved back to town."

"I moved away the day of graduation. It took my father's imminent death to bring me back . . . and it didn't take long for this guy to swoop me off my feet."

"So he's a good swooper?" Sammy asked.

"The best!"

Barry frowned. "Maybe I could take lessons on swooping from you, Austin. Have you ever given them formally?"

"I think your heart just has to be one-hundred percent committed to the swoopee for it to work."

Dallas sighed. "If I were an English teacher, I'd be *very* offended right now."

"It's a good thing you teach math, dear," Austin said with a grin.

Sammy sat back, watching the other three talk for a few minutes. She had never really thought of Dallas in any way other than as a patient, so she was surprised how much she was liking her in this social situation. "We need to have lunch together sometime soon," Sammy said to Dallas.

"I'd love that. I don't have a lot of female friends in town. I've been a little too obsessed with a certain man to make friends here since I returned. I'm friends with the wives of his two closest friends but no one else really."

"I can understand that completely. I've had nothing but time, so I have a few female friends."

"Well, and your job puts you in touch with all of the women in town. That's quite different than talking to every teenager in high school." Dallas shook her head. "Sometimes I'll do anything for a little adult conversation."

"Next time you feel that way, just give me a call. We'll leave Austin with the baby and run away and do something fun. Like go to the bookstore and try to nag Barry into expanding his romance section."

Dallas laughed. "We'll have to dig through each other's romance collections as well. I'm sure I'll find something I want to read in yours, and you should find something in mine."

"Remember there's a bookseller at the table. None of this book-swapping now!" Barry said with a laugh.

The band started playing again, and all of them gravitated back to the dance floor. Sammy was happy. She'd not only started dating a man she was very attracted to, but she had made a new friend of an old acquaintance. Why had they never realized how much they had in common before?

It was a little after ten when Sammy finally said, "I need to get home. I have to be ready for any deliveries that may come, and I need to plan to have the clinic open tomorrow. Everyone knows I live there, so snow or no snow, I'm stuck!"

Barry nodded. "I can take you home." He couldn't believe how much he wanted the night to go on and on. Usually when he dated someone new, they were clinging to him and not the other way around.

Sammy hugged Dallas before leaving. "Remember to call me when you need adult conversation. I would love to hang out with you sometime soon."

Dallas smiled. "I'll do that!"

The whole drive home, Sammy had a slight smile on her face. The snow was coming down hard and heavy, and there were a couple of places when she was sure Barry's four-wheel drive wouldn't be enough to get them through the snow. She was worried he really would have to use the snow plow on the front of his truck.

When they got to her home, he got out of the truck and walked around to help her down. "I had a wonderful time," he said. "I hope you'll go out with me again soon."

Sammy nodded. "I really enjoyed myself. You just let me know when, and I'll be there."

He had his hand on her arm, and she could feel it burning through her thick, winter coat. When they got to her door, he turned to her. "About that kiss . . ."

"Is it as romantic if you talk about it first?" she asked, frowning at him.

"I'm not sure. I guess I should change the subject. How do you think the Cubs will do this year?"

"Cubs?" she asked. "You mean the baseball team?"

While she still had a look of confusion on her face, he leaned down and brushed his lips against hers.

Taken by surprise, Sammy stood there for a moment before wrapping her arms around Barry's neck and holding on for dear life. His mouth moved against hers in a way that had her moving closer to him. Whoever had taught him to kiss had done an excellent job.

When he finally lifted his head, her lips were swollen from his kiss, and her eyes were half closed. "That was amazing," she said softly.

He smiled. "I'll call you. Maybe we can go out tomorrow night."

"I need to get the last details put together for my sister's shower. We're doing it here in the clinic, so I'll be decorating all night."

"Maybe I'll come help then. I can bring a pizza."

She smiled. "That would make me happier than I could express." She looked up at him, trying to memorize how his face looked with the snow clinging to his eyelashes. "I sometimes have to cancel at the last minute for deliveries. I hope you'll keep that in mind."

"I understand." He leaned down and kissed her once more, quickly. "Hurry in before you freeze to death."

"You would never let me freeze in your arms."

"I think I like you." He turned and rushed back to his truck, while she opened the door and went inside.

She changed into her pajamas, went into her bedroom, and realized she heard a snow plow. Looking out the window, she saw Barry was plowing her parking lot for her. It would be covered again by morning, but he'd made her job so much easier. The man was something special. There was no doubt about it.

* * *

Sammy called in a to-go order at Bob's the following day, so she would have time to run to the bakery and pick up the cake for the baby shower. When she walked into the bakery and saw the cake for the first time, she put her hand over her mouth in surprise. "You outdid yourself this time, Grace. It's beautiful!"

The cake depicted Tabby, stethoscope around her neck, and a zippered tummy with a baby popping out. Tabby actually looked like herself, and Sammy couldn't be more excited.

Grace grinned at her. She was the younger sister of the Quinlan Quads and half of the Quinlan twins. "I'm so glad you like it! I used a picture of Tabby that I had, and I made it look as much like her as I could. It was so fun, and a challenge for me."

"I'm glad you had fun with it. It looks amazing." Sammy paid for the cake. "You're going to be there tomorrow, right?"

Grace nodded. "I wouldn't miss it for the world."

Patience nodded from behind Grace. "I'll be there, too. So will Felicity."

"Where is Felicity today?" Sammy asked. The girl rarely missed work.

"She and Allen are looking at houses with Megan. They decided to get something bigger, since she's having twins this time. It's hard to believe how big our family has gotten since we moved here," Patience said.

"Well, good for them! Thanks so much for your help." Sammy headed for the door, nodding to the man opening it. She didn't recognize him, but that wasn't surprising. All of the new commerce in Culpepper had brought in a lot of strangers from surrounding areas.

"Thank you," she said as she hurried to her car with the cake.

As soon as she got home, she dug into her taco burger and fried cheese curds, smiling contentedly. She wasn't sure what it was about the combination, but they sure made her happy.

As she was eating, she got a call, swallowed quickly, and answered. "Hello?"

"How's my favorite single daughter?"

"Hey, Mom. What's up?"

"Well, I think I told you I'm dating a great guy . . ."

Sammy frowned. Something was up, and she had a feeling she didn't want to be any part of it. "Sure. He's a plumber there in Cheyenne."

"Right! Well, he has a son around your age . . ."

"Mom, I'm dating someone." It felt so good to be able to tell her mother that. Sure, they weren't serious and had only been on one date so far, but at least she wouldn't have to deal with her mother's matchmaking.

"But . . . I'm sure you'd like Scott . . ."

"Mom, I'm finally taking the bull by the horns and writing my own story. No more blind dates. Ever. Barry and I went out last night, and he's coming over again tonight to help me decorate for Tabby's shower. Are you coming, by the way? She would love to have you here."

"I'm planning to be there. Are you sure I can't bring Scott for you to meet?"

Sammy shook her head. She loved her mother, but at times, she was altogether too pushy. "I'm sure. Even if I wasn't dating someone, I wouldn't have time tomorrow anyway. I'm playing hostess for Tabby's shower. Remember?" At first, she had hoped her mother would help her throw it, but it was clear that wasn't happening.

"I remember. All right, I'll leave him at home. See you tomorrow evening."

"Bye, Mom. Love you!"

"Love you, too!"

After ending the call, Sammy sighed. What was wrong with her? She hoped the idea of her meeting this Scott was out of her mother's head now. She didn't need to worry about being set up with a stranger. She was busy enough as it was.

She quickly finished her lunch and washed her hands. She had a patient in fifteen minutes. Thankfully the plows had made short work of the roads, and everything had been business as usual all day.

***

True to his word, Barry was there just before six that evening. He held a pizza box in his hands. Sammy opened the door wide before he had a chance to knock. "Hey you!" She took the box from him and carried it over to the counter.

Barry looked around the space of her home. "This is nice."

She smiled. "It's a lot nicer now that it's just me. It was a little cramped when I shared it with Tabby."

"You two are close, I take it?"

Sammy nodded. "Yeah, she's a year older than me, and we have always been super close. We love that we have been able to work so closely together." She took down plates and forks, setting some napkins on the counter. "I only have Sprite in my fridge. You okay with that? Or water, of course. Milk."

"Sprite's fine. I like to have pop with my pizza." He wouldn't have gone to all the fuss of getting plates and forks for pizza, but he didn't complain, simply putting a couple of pieces on the plate she handed him. "I'm starving. I wasn't sure what you liked on your pizza, so I told the little pizza place in town to just give me whatever you usually get."

She laughed, looking at the pizza. "I wondered how you knew! Small towns." The pizza was her exact order. Canadian bacon, sausage, and mushrooms.

"Yup. It wouldn't have worked anywhere bigger than this." He took his plate to the table and sat down, waiting for her to come with her own pizza. She set her plate down and got them each a bottle of Sprite from the fridge.

"I'm so hungry! I'm glad you got here when you did." She took a bite of the pizza and wiped her mouth with her napkin. She loved pizza, but it was tough on a date because it was so messy.

"I'm pretty darn hungry, too. We'll eat this and then work on decorations. Do you have any idea what you have in mind?"

"Yeah, I have balloons, a helium tank, and streamers. It's going to be all decked out in blue because she's having a boy. I want to make her favorite office chair her throne and have streamers floating to the floor. Should be fun."

"Sounds good to me. As soon as we're done eating, we're going to conquer it."

Chapter 4

Working with Barry that night, Sammy realized just how well they fit together. It took them two hours to completely transform the waiting room of the clinic into a balloon and streamer-ridden party room.

"Once the cake is in place, it's going to look perfect!" Sammy said, standing back and looking at everything.

"You think?" he asked.

She nodded. "Yeah, it looks just like a baby shower should." She plopped down in one of the chairs in the waiting room. "What do you think?"

He shrugged. "I don't think I'm allowed to have an opinion. I've never been to a baby shower!"

Sammy laughed. "I go to almost every baby shower in town because they're all either for my patients or Tabby's, and a lot of times, they're both."

"Well, if you think it looks good, it must be perfect, then."

"Yes, definitely perfect." She sighed happily. "Our mom is coming here from Cheyenne tomorrow. Not sure if I'm ready."

"Why's that?" he asked, frowning at her.

"Well, she called today during my lunch and wanted to bring with her the son of the man she's dating. She is always trying to set me up with someone. I told her I was dating and made it seem a whole lot more serious than it really is, just to get her out of my hair."

"How serious did you make it seem?" Barry asked. He would happily make anything she'd said a reality.

"More serious than one date, for sure. I didn't really give any details, though, so she can infer what she will."

Barry turned to her. "I'm pretty serious. I mean, I know we've only gone out once, but . . . I'm developing feelings for you pretty darn quick."

Sammy felt her heart beat faster at his words. "Really?"

He nodded. "Really. I've never dated anyone like you." He gave a short laugh. "I don't know if I've ever dated much, to be honest. Most of the girls I went out with were rodeo groupies, if that makes sense. They'd follow the rodeo from one place to the next, hoping to get them a roper."

"Why?" Sammy asked. She'd never understood that kind of lifestyle.

"Because we're all sexy and seven feet tall, of course," he replied.

"How did I not know that?" she asked.

"No clue."

She grinned, walking back toward her place from the clinic. "I'm going to have another piece of pizza. My way of celebrating the decorating being done."

"Are you just serving cake tomorrow? Are there other goodies we can get into?"

She laughed. "Well, I'm doing punch and chips and dip and a few other snacky things. People will eat before they come, though, so no meals or anything."

"Do you cook?" he asked.

"Are you asking me to cook for you at ten at night? 'Cuz I'm not doing it."

He laughed. "No, I was just curious if you cook at all. I wouldn't ask anyone to cook for me at this hour of the night. Not even my mother. Of course, she never could cook anyway, so I can't imagine asking her to cook anything."

"Huh. My mom cooked a lot, but then the parents divorced. I think she still cooks. I haven't stayed with her in a long time."

"Well, you do kind of have your own life to live."

"I do! I'm so glad you can see that!" She put the pizza back onto the counter from the fridge. "Want it cold, or should I heat it in the oven?"

"Why not nuke it?"

"Dries it out too much. If I'm going to reheat pizza, I'll *always* do it in the oven."

He shrugged, bowing to her superior experience in pizza reheating. "Let's eat it cold." He grabbed a piece and put it on the plate she had set out. Why did women feel the need to eat pizza on a plate? "You never did answer my question. Do you cook?"

She nodded. "I'm actually a really good cook. I prefer *not* to cook, but I can do it and do it well when the situation calls for it."

He eyed her suspiciously. "So you don't cook daily?"

She shrugged. "I heat stuff up daily. I tend to make a big pot of soup on Sundays and munch on it all week. If I crave something, I'll make it during the week, but for the most part, I only really cook on the weekends. I eat out for lunch every day because Bob cooks for me."

"You seem to think a lot of Bob. Do I have reason to be jealous there?"

She laughed. "Megan would kill me if I tried something with Bob. She's tiny but fierce!"

He grinned. "I haven't had the pleasure of meeting Megan yet."

"She's a real estate agent here in town, and she and Bob are a perfect fit. She's pregnant with their second child, and I'm going to deliver it. I delivered their first, too."

"Sounds like Megan is someone I want to meet, then. I think a lot of Bob. He's sent lots of customers my way."

"Sounds like Bob. He's a good guy, even though he tries to come across as grumpy all the time. I think he has in his head that good chefs have to be grumpy."

"They don't?"

She shook her head. "They really don't. Not at all." She shrugged, thinking about what she needed to do next. "I'm making four different kinds of dips for the party tomorrow. Some are cooked, and some aren't. And I'm making cookies, though they won't hold a candle to Patience Jenner's cookies. She's amazing!"

"I've heard interesting things about Patience, I'm afraid. She sounds like a real character."

"Oh, she is. Don't doubt that, but she's fun and hilarious. I really like her." Sammy shrugged. "And she's a good customer. I've delivered one baby, and now she's pregnant with twins!"

He laughed. "I guess you're not a fan of birth control."

"Well, on some levels I am . . ." She grinned at him. "So how's the book business? Are you doing well?"

He shrugged. "I've only been open for a week, but I was hoping for better from my first week. I sure hope everyone is right and sales will pick up during the summer months. I'm not sure I'll be able to keep it going otherwise."

She frowned. "Well, I think we desperately need a bookstore here in town, so I will do my best to support you. If you want to print up flyers or coupons of some sort, I'll put them in the waiting room."

"That's not a bad idea. I wonder if Bob would do the same."

"I think half the businesses in town would. Want me to talk to Grace about it tomorrow? She and her cousins own the bakery, and they'll be here."

"That would be wonderful, if you don't mind. I hope you know I'm not dating you for your local business connections."

She laughed. "If you were, you'd be silly. Everyone in town has the same connections."

"I guess that's true." He finished his pizza and wiped his mouth. "So tomorrow night you have the shower, right?"

"I do. My whole day will be wrapped up in shower activities, like cooking and getting the games set up."

"What about Sunday?"

She shrugged. "I usually do my laundry after church, but I could probably work that fascinating activity into my cooking day tomorrow." She shook her head. "This was a bad week for us to start dating with Tabby's shower tomorrow."

"Well, how would you feel about going sledding after church? Or snowmobiling? Or we could hang out in my bookstore. Or I could take you to a movie? I guess I'm trying to say that I want to spend the day with you."

"I'd like to spend the day with you, too!" Sammy shrugged. "Any of those activities would be good, as far as I'm concerned."

"I think it's supposed to be a little cold for outdoor stuff. Why don't we see a movie?"

"What's playing?" she asked.

"I really don't care," Barry said with a grin. "I just want to spend the day with you."

She laughed. "Well, then let's go see whatever's playing and have a good day." She loved that he didn't care what movie it was. It made her feel like she was the main attraction, and every woman should feel that way.

"All right! I haven't been to church yet since moving here, and I think I'm going to go on Sunday. May I sit with you?"

She blinked a couple of times. "You know that in a town like this, sitting with me at church is like announcing we're not only dating, we're engaged, I'm pregnant, and the marriage will be taking place within the next few days, right?"

He laughed. "I don't care. Do you?"

"Well, I don't necessarily want to be pregnant with your child after only knowing you a couple of days. . . . Let me think on it!"

He shook his head. "I think we should go sit together on the couch."

"Why? Because you want me closer so you can grope me? I'm not sure my daddy would approve."

He grinned. "Your daddy isn't here, little girl."

She threw back her head and laughed. "You sounded so lecherous for a moment there!"

He stood up and took her hand, pulling her with him to her couch. "There, now we're right where we should be." His arm went around her shoulders, and he just held her close. She had a fire going in the fireplace in front of them. "I like your little place."

"Me too. Tabby and I designed it together when we built the clinic. It feels like home for sure. I do like the extra space now that she's gone."

"Isn't she married to one of the O'Donnells?"

"She is. To Arch. He's the architect of the family."

"What does Arch stand for?"

She giggled. "Archibald. Tabby likes to torment him with his full name on occasion. It makes her happy."

He shook his head. "Well, you can never torment me with my full name, all right?"

"What's your full name?" She turned toward him, only then realizing just how close they were sitting.

"Bartholomew. And that will not be repeated. You hear me?"

She giggled. "I hear you. I really do. I like it, though. And I'm really Samantha. My parents were really into the old TV show *Bewitched,* so they named my sister and me Samantha and Tabitha. I think it's silly, but no one really makes the connection."

"Hmm . . . Samantha. That sounds so much more girly than Sammy does."

She grinned. "I've always been Sammy. From the time I was able to walk, they'd already shortened it. And Tabby has always been Tabby."

"Well, I like Sammy. It suits you." He leaned down and quickly brushed his lips across hers. "I like kissing Sammy, too."

"I approve of your choice of activities." She wiggled her eyebrows at him even as she leaned in for another longer, deeper kiss. She'd never imagined she'd be still single in her thirties, having make out sessions on her couch. What was wrong with her?

His hands gripped her waist and pulled her in closer to him. "You are absolutely intoxicating, Sammy Jo."

She pulled away. "How did you know that my middle name is Jo?"

He shrugged. "Just seems to fit you!"

"Hmmm . . . have you been checking up on me, Bartholomew James?"

"My middle name is not James."

"Then what is it? You already know my middle name is Jo."

He wrinkled his nose. "I'd rather not say."

"That bad, huh? Is it Melvin?"

He laughed. "I'm not telling, so you can quit trying to force it out of me. Bartholomew is bad enough without the middle name added in."

"Well, I hardly think you should be ashamed of your name. What happened to your father?" She knew the change in subject must seem abrupt, but he'd mentioned his mother after the divorce, but never his father.

"My dad enlisted in the marines after they divorced. He's gone on and had a new family entirely. New wife. Four kids. I don't fit in with them. He always paid child support, but he never had any desire to see me."

"That's sad. So you don't really have a relationship with him?"

He shook his head. "It's really how my mom wanted it, to be honest. She thought whatever man she was married to at the time should be my father. Period. It was weird."

"That does sound weird. Did you make any kind of connection with any of the men?"

"Just with Bart's dad. After him, I didn't even try. I was tired of having father figures in and out of my life."

"I can understand that." Sammy rested her head on his shoulder, wishing there was a way she could heal all of his childhood hurts. "Tell me about the rodeo."

He shrugged. "I drove from one city to the next to be part of rodeos. I'd be in the heat of Texas in the summer, and the next week in a small town in Idaho. It was ridiculous. I loved it, though. I loved the cheer of the crowd. I loved the feeling of riding that bronco. I probably would still be doing it if I hadn't injured my leg so badly. It's full of ugly scars."

"Chicks dig scars. Didn't you ever see *The Replacements?*"

He laughed. "I'll keep that in mind. Are you a chick?"

"I wouldn't say that. Other girls are. I don't think I want to be a chick, though."

"Yeah, I always thought the term was derogatory."

"It is. Sort of." She glanced at the clock, wondering how much longer he'd stay. She needed to be up early if she was going to do everything that needed to be done before the shower.

"Are you ready for me to go?" he asked, noting that she looked at the clock.

"I kind of want you to stay forever, but I have to be up early to get everything done tomorrow." She shook her head. "So what do I say? Please don't go, but let me sleep?"

He laughed, kissing her softly. "I'll go, and I'll see you Sunday. I may even go to the bar tomorrow night and check out that darts tournament. Could be fun."

She smiled. "Did I remember to thank you for plowing my parking lot? You made my day yesterday so much easier. I think I really do like you."

He frowned. "You loved me on Wednesday. How did I get downgraded to really do like on Friday! I need to work on my moves." He got to his feet and pulled her to hers. "Should I start reading romance novels?"

She laughed. "I loved the store before I loved you. See? Now that I'm getting to know you, I have to start from like."

"But I want you to go back to love. That was more fun for me."

Sammy stood on tiptoe and kissed him goodnight after he'd put his coat on. "I'll see you at church on Sunday. Get ready for a wild ride." She grinned. "Well, unless Ben is preaching, and he might be. He almost seems sane when he gives the sermon."

"Almost seems sane? I need to hear Brother Anthony, don't I?"

"You sure do." She stood at the door and watched him rush out through the falling snow to his truck.

After closing the door, she sighed. He was growing on her pretty darn fast. Much faster than she'd thought he would. The man was a booklover, and he kissed like a dream. No wonder she was falling for him so fast.

She took a quick shower and brushed her teeth, her mind on nothing but the man who had just left. He was pretty darn special to her, and she didn't know how to even express it. She'd known him for only three days, and already she was falling for him.

What was the world coming to when boring Sammy Ross was falling in love with a man she'd just met? The news would be earth shattering to anyone who knew her well.

After finishing getting ready for bed, she climbed under the covers and reached for one of the books she'd purchased at his store. She was already making a list of the authors she wanted him to carry and how the whole romance section should be set up. With more romance novels, she was certain more women would shop there, and his store would be more successful. He just needed to listen to her.

She read a chapter and then grabbed the pen and paper that were always on her nightstand, quickly making a list of everything she had to do the next day. She'd do laundry all day and make the dips. She had to make the punch. And . . . she was getting tired just thinking about it all. Why had she volunteered to throw this baby shower? Someone else should have done it.

She shut off the light, and her last thought before she fell asleep was about Barry. His brown eyes were sparkling as he kissed her before leaving. She hoped she would always remember him just that way. Her

Barry. Whether she'd lost her mind or not, she planned to marry the man. She just hadn't told him yet.

Across town, Barry climbed into his own bed, his mind entirely consumed by Sammy. She was something special, and he knew he was going to have to keep her. He wondered how long he needed to wait after meeting her before he could propose? Probably more than three days, but did it have to be more than a week? He hoped not. Maybe he'd call his mother for advice.

Shaking his head, he shut off the light. Like his mother gave good advice about anything.

Chapter 5

The clinic was hopping the following evening with all of the women the sisters had helped with their babies and so many more. Tabby was overwhelmed by all of the attention and had tears in her eyes more than once.

Sammy played hostess, hurrying back and forth between the clinic and the kitchen, refilling dips and talking to everyone.

When the party was finally over, several of the women stayed behind to help clean up, including all eight of the Quinlans, as well as Dallas. As all of the women worked, they laughed and talked about what it would be like for a midwife to deliver an obstetrician's baby.

Tabby looked at Sammy. "It's going to go beautifully, and we do have an obstetrician standing by to do a c-section, just in case."

Sammy shrugged. "I don't think it'll be necessary, but I do like to always have someone standing by. Usually, it's my sister, but . . ."

"We're going to do great!"

Dallas turned to Sammy. "Who's going to assist you, though? Doesn't Tabby usually assist you, and you usually assist her?"

"Yeah, that's how it's done. I don't know. Do you want to help?" Sammy grinned. She knew she could do it on her own, but it was fun watching other women get flustered.

"I would *love* to!" Dallas said, looking excited.

Sammy was surprised, but when she looked at Tabby, her sister nodded. "You're in, apparently!"

"I love that sort of thing! I almost went into medicine, but teaching is what drew my heart."

"Well, we'll be thrilled for the help," Tabby said. "She thinks she can do it alone, but I know we will need another pair of hands."

Sammy rolled her eyes. She'd delivered babies alone before, and she would again. It would be nice not to have to, though. "Sounds good to me. I'll be glad to have an assistant."

Patricia Ross walked over then, kissing each of her girls on the cheek. "I don't see a ring on your finger, Sammy. If you change your mind, let me know."

"Thanks, Mom. I will."

Patricia hurried out the door then, and Tabby turned on Sammy. "Ring on your finger?"

"Mom's trying to set me up with her new boyfriend's son. I told her I'm seeing someone, and she still wanted to set me up. That's all."

"You're seeing someone?" Tabby asked. *"Seriously* seeing someone?"

Sammy shrugged. "I'm not sure how serious we are yet, but I like him a lot."

Dallas stepped closer. "They were adorable together at the Watering Hole the other night. They danced and danced."

"Sounds like there might be something serious going on. Is it time for me to trick the two of you into getting married?" Tabby asked. She'd held that same threat over Sammy for over two years.

"You're happy, sis. Let me find my *own* happiness." Sammy picked up an armful of baby gifts. "Want me to take these out to your amazing new mommyvan?"

"Oh, hush. You know you have minivan envy! And yes, please!"

Everyone who was still there picked up an armload of gifts and took them to the car, each of them hugging Tabby.

"You're going to be an amazing mother," Felicity said. "I'm so excited for you!" Their bellies bumped as they hugged. Felicity's was bigger than Tabby's, though Tabby was much closer to her due date.

Tabby looked at Felicity. "I know Sammy is delivering the twins, but I'd like to do one more sonogram before my baby is born, if you don't mind. There are more likely to be complications with twins, and I want to make sure everything is all right."

Felicity nodded. "Sure. I love peeking at the little monsters."

Sammy grinned. "You should name them Bert and Ernie."

"Don't think I haven't thought about it!" Felicity winked at Sammy before hurrying away. "See you in church tomorrow! And I'll make an appointment first thing Monday morning, Tabby!"

When it was just the two sisters left, Tabby hurried back inside, and Sammy followed. "I want to know everything about the guy you're dating."

Sammy shrugged. "He is the owner of the new bookstore in town, next to Bob's Burger Barn. I told you I was going out with him."

"You told me you were going to go on one date with him. You're 'seeing each other' now?"

"It seems to be moving along pretty fast. He brought pizza last night, and he stayed and helped me decorate. He plowed the parking lot on Thursday night when he thought I wasn't watching." Sammy frowned. "I don't know where we're going if we're going anywhere, but I think a lot of him, and he gets my motor running, if you know what I mean."

Tabby laughed. "I know *exactly* what you mean. Well, I want to be kept in the loop. Don't run off and get married without me."

"I won't. How could I? You're my favorite sister."

"Wasn't I your least favorite sister the other day?"

"Both. You are definitely both."

"Well, I'm leaving you, then. Is everything cleaned up enough?" Tabby looked around her, making sure all the trash was thrown away and they weren't leaving Sammy with a huge mess to clean up.

"Definitely. I'm good from here. And I need to get to bed, because church is tomorrow."

"Are you seeing Barry tomorrow?"

Sammy blushed. "He's going to sit with me at church—"

"That's huge!"

"And then we're going to see a movie. Probably get lunch. I'm not sure what all we'll do, but whatever it is, we'll be doing it together."

"I can't wait to meet the man that makes my sister blush like she's sixteen again. That's so awesome!"

Sammy smiled and watched her sister hurry out to her mommyvan. "Be careful on the ice! I don't want to deliver that baby tonight!"

"You won't! I'm careful!"

As Tabby drove away, Sammy thought about how very happy she was for her sister and the love she'd found with Arch. Hopefully, that love was just around the corner for her.

* * *

Sammy had just about decided that Barry wasn't going to come to church when he slid into the pew beside her. "Morning," he whispered softly. His jeans had been traded in for a pair of slacks, and he wore a cowboy tie. He looked good to Sammy.

"G'morning. I figured you weren't coming," she whispered back.

"Nah. I just had to find my dress boots. They were in a box in the top of my closet. How did they get there?"

Sammy shrugged, turning to the front as Pastor Ben walked up to the pulpit. She wasn't sure if she should be happy or disappointed that Barry wasn't going to be treated to the full Brother Anthony special service.

The talk that week was on forgiveness, something everyone needed, in Sammy's opinion. It was hard not to hold a grudge against people who had done her wrong, and she was sure others were the same.

After the service, several different couples surrounded them. Sammy met Dallas's eyes across the room, and she hoped that the other woman would see her silent plea.

Felicity was there, introducing Barry to Allen. "Barry owns the bookstore here in town."

Allen nodded. "I did most of the renovations on the building. We've been working together for months. Hi, Barry."

Barry grinned. "Hey."

Finally, Dallas came over and smiled at Sammy. "Barry, you remember Austin, and this is our daughter, Odessa."

Barry nodded. "It's good to see you." It was obvious the other couple was rescuing them from the swarm of people around them.

Austin asked, "Are you still planning to have lunch with us?" He held little Odessa in his arms. Since both of them were named after Texas cities, they had to follow the tradition with their daughter.

"Yes!" Sammy answered for both of them. She was thrilled with the excuse to get away from prying eyes.

As they left the church, she breathed a sigh of relief. "I didn't think we'd ever get out of there."

Barry laughed. "They were definitely interested in who I was."

"I told you sitting next to me would be almost like announcing our engagement." Sammy shook her head. "Small towns are notorious for situations like that."

"I see," he said, wrapping his arm around her shoulders. "What would happen if I kissed you in the church parking lot? Would you then be pregnant with my child?"

Dallas laughed. "She would!"

"Oh no!" Barry said, grinning at Sammy.

Sammy sighed. "You joke about it, but it's *my* reputation on the line here."

"Yeah, you'd be a slut, but I'd just be a ladies' man."

The five of them headed to the diner to eat and sat down in a booth off to one side of the room. Odessa sat in a high chair, eating crackers. While they ate, Sammy asked Dallas about the type of romance she liked, and they talked a lot. Austin talked animatedly with Barry about the rodeo, and it became a men's discussion and a women's discussion.

After they'd eaten, Barry took Sammy's hand. "We're going to head to the movies."

"What's playing?" Austin asked.

Barry shrugged. "Who cares as long as we can sit in the back row and make out?"

"Not in front of my baby!" Dallas said with a laugh.

"She's a cutie." Barry reached out and toyed with her fingers.

Odessa pulled away and buried her face in her mother's shoulder.

"I delivered her," Sammy said softly.

"You did?" Barry looked at Sammy, connecting what she did now. "I guess I knew you delivered babies, but until I saw one you'd brought into the world, it didn't really hit home."

"I can believe that." Sammy grinned at him, so glad he was there with her.

"We need to get this one home for a nap," Dallas said with a yawn. "And maybe her mama, too."

"Definitely her mama, too! All mothers need naps."

Dallas laughed. "Did you hear that, Austin? I need a nap."

Austin reached over and took Odessa. "Let's get home. Enjoy your movie, if you ever figure out what it is."

"Oh, trust me. We will!"

Sammy shook her head as they walked away. "I can't believe you told them we were going to sit in the back row and make out. What were you thinking?"

Barry shrugged. "I figured they'd understand completely." He led her to his truck, and they drove the short distance to the movie theater. "Is this one of the businesses that Sly owns?"

"I have no idea. I cannot keep up with everything that man is buying in this town. He's crazy!"

He bought two tickets for "anything but a kid movie." Sammy couldn't believe he'd actually put it that way.

"People are really going to think we're here to sit in the back and make out!"

"Well, I got the impression you weren't ready for things to go to the next level, and if we spend too much time alone, I'm sure they will. So we'll sit at the back of the movie theater and make out there instead of at your place or mine. Much less dangerous."

She couldn't believe him, but she couldn't think of a good response either. "I don't even know what to say to that!"

"Thank me for sparing your morals," he said, leading her into the theater, where he handed her a bucket of popcorn and her drink.

"Are we going to be able to eat popcorn and drink pop if we're too busy making out?" she asked.

A woman two rows ahead of them turned around and glared at her. Sammy was mortified. "I'm kidding!" she called out.

"No she's not!" Barry said.

"You're making me crazy, Barry!"

"That's okay. You make me crazy, too." He put his arm around her and dug a hand into the popcorn tub she was holding. "Did you catch the name of the movie we're seeing?"

The woman turned and glared at them again. Sammy knew her because she was one of the checkers at the grocery store.

"Stop that!" Sammy hissed at Barry.

He shrugged. "We'll figure it out. Maybe."

She shook her head. "I'm not sure I'm going to agree to be seen in public with you after today."

"All right. I'll be alone with you all you want . . ."

"That wasn't what I meant and you know it."

"I'll take it how I want to take it. And I like my way an awful lot."

"Of course you do . . ."

* * *

After the movie—Sammy still had no idea what she'd seen, but she knew she'd annoyed the blond checker from the supermarket—they went to his truck. "I can't believe you embarrassed me like that!"

"I can't believe you spent the entire movie with your lips glued to mine," Barry said, shaking his head. "I thought better of you than that."

"What movie did we see anyway?"

"Does it really matter?"

She laughed helplessly. "Until today, I thought you were this really nice guy, and now I realize you're like all other men."

"Nah. Don't say that!" He clutched his chest with one hand, acting as if she'd broken his heart.

"I do like you, Barry Hamilton. You make me see the world in totally new ways."

"Or not see it at all, because you're too busy kissing me to care about it as it passes you by?"

"That could be true . . ." She sighed. "So are you dumping me at my truck now?" She wasn't quite ready for the day to end, but she needed to be mindful of her work the next day.

"I have not yet begun to date you!"

"And that means . . ."

"It means I think we should go back to your place. We can just spend time together. Watch a movie, maybe . . ."

Sammy let out a bark of laughter. "I just tried to watch a movie! I don't know anything that happened in it!"

"That's because you weren't paying attention." He shook his head. "I can't take you anywhere . . ."

"Okay, we'll go back to my place. Take me to my truck, though, so I will have it when I need it."

"I don't know if I can be apart from you for that long!" The back of his hand went to his forehead, and he sighed dramatically for effect.

"You'll have to be, because I'll need my truck tomorrow."

"All right. All right. I'll take you to your truck. Are you going to cook supper for me while we watch our movie?"

"Sure. I have nothing better to do."

Barry smiled. "I was hoping you'd say that!" He drove her to the church's parking lot and left her at her truck. "There. Happy now?"

"Sure. Why wouldn't I be?" Sammy blew a kiss as she got out of his truck and rushed to her own. The snow had finally stopped, but it was bitter cold. "See you at my place!"

She got into her truck and started it, letting it heat up for a few minutes before leaving the parking lot. The whole time, she was very aware that he was right behind her and watching everything she said and did.

She pulled into the small parking lot of the clinic and jumped out, running to the door with her key, so she could get where it was warm. She hadn't been warm since the theater, since both trucks had been cold. Inside, she hurried to the fireplace and started a fire, hearing him come in and close the door.

"I'll start the fire while you start supper," he offered.

"Almost done," she replied, standing up from the fireplace. "Soup okay? I was thinking of a thick baked potato soup tonight. I have bacon and cheese for it as well."

He nodded emphatically. "Sounds delicious. I'll figure out what movie we should watch."

"Let's not spend money on a movie you have no intentions of watching," she said, shaking her head.

"We'll watch it!" he protested, knowing full well they wouldn't. There was something about little Samantha Ross that made his blood boil.

"Fine, find a movie, and I will get supper started. I have Netflix, and it's already signed on. And Amazon Prime. And Hulu."

"You sure do love your streaming services."

"I hate trying to watch network television. It's cheaper to have all of those services and watch whatever I want when I want." She pulled potatoes out of a container on her counter and ran water over them before peeling them.

"Let me see what you like, and I'll go from there." Barry sat down with her remote and started pushing buttons. He wasn't a huge fan of smart TVs, because they were usually smarter than he was, but he'd give it a try.

Thirty minutes later when she sat beside him while the potatoes boiled, he turned on the show he'd chosen. "You had this on Amazon, so I figured we'd watch it together."

She laughed. "I have it memorized!"

"Who doesn't? This way we won't worry about missing the movie." The opening credits for *The Princess Bride* rolled across the screen, and she snuggled into his side contentedly.

"I wanted to marry Westley when I was a little girl."

"You did? Not Prince Humperdinck?"

"Oh, please. He was the villain of the story. Well, him and Count Rugan. No one wanted either of them. They were evil."

"Shh . . . this is the part where she calls him farm boy and he goes off to find his fortune."

"But he's kidnapped by the Dread Pirate Roberts, and the Dread Pirate Roberts never takes a prisoner!"

He shook his head. "You have seen this show one too many times. I don't want you to be bored, though . . ."

"You don't?"

He shook his head and grabbed her by the waist, pulling her close to him. "I'll distract you."

And he did. Very well, actually. Within moments, she forgot about the soup, the movie, and everything else around her. She only existed for his touch and his kisses.

Chapter 6

Sammy had her arms wrapped around him, and she sat in Barry's lap. They were kissing one another for all they were worth. As they kissed, she heard an incessant beeping that she ignored—at first. After a bit, she lifted her head. "The soup!" She jumped off his lap and ran into the kitchen. "It's not burning."

"I am," Barry mumbled. He took deep gulping breaths, trying to calm his raging libido.

"I'm sorry!" she said, hating that she'd run from him so quickly, but she hated when something was scorched into a pan. It had happened more than once while she delivered babies, and it was so hard to clean up.

He walked to the other side of the counter where she was cooking, leaning on it. "What would it take to talk you into marrying me?" he asked. He hadn't quite realized the words were about to pop out of his mouth, but . . . he was glad when they did.

At first, her heart skipped a beat, but then Sammy laughed, stirring the thickening for the soup. "We've known one another for what? Five days? Time to marry!"

"I'm serious, Sammy. I've never felt this much for anyone, and I don't know that I can keep seeing you like this. Not without dragging you off to bed, and I don't think that's who you are."

She frowned. "It's not who I am. I've never . . . not before marriage."

"That's what I thought. So, let's get married. Tomorrow. What's the waiting period in Wyoming?" Barry looked so serious, Sammy almost believed he meant it.

"If you'd lived here more than a few months, you'd know the answer. There is no waiting period. Everyone is running around getting married in three hours around here. It's absolutely crazy." She stirred the thickening into the soup and brought it to a boil, turning down the heat. Walking to the fridge, she removed the grated cheese and put some bacon on a microwave bacon tray, covering it with a paper towel. "Do you want butter and sour cream?"

"Yes, but listen to me. I'm not kidding. Marry me. Tomorrow!"

"We can't get married just because we can't keep our hands off each other. That would be crazy. Where would we be in six months after the passion wore off?" Sammy tried to talk sense into him, but she wasn't sure if she was convincing him or herself. She so badly just wanted to agree and let the chips fall where they may.

"The passion isn't going to wear off. I guarantee it."

"You can't! After five days' acquaintance, you're that certain we should be married? Really?"

He nodded. "I *am* that certain. Please, Sammy, marry me."

She frowned. "I have appointments all day. There's no time to plan a wedding."

"Sure, there is. You can get all the women whose babies you've delivered involved. I'm sure there are dresses for the borrowing. Come on. It won't hurt anything. And you said you wanted me to see a wedding performed by Brother Anthony? What better wedding than our own?"

She laughed. He had no idea what he was getting into there. "If I said yes, you'd freak out."

"No, I wouldn't." Barry shook his head. "Look, I've lived the wild nomadic life. I came here to Culpepper to settle down. I wanted to own my own store and hopefully find a woman to marry and have children with. You are my *destiny*. I closed my eyes and pointed on a map, and Culpepper is the place that I pointed to. This is where providence brought me."

"So you're saying we're fated to marry, because this is the town you poked on a map with your eyes closed?" Sammy wondered if she shouldn't call in a psychiatrist. The man sounded like he was losing his mind.

He shook his head. "That's not all there is to it, and you know it. I believe we're meant to be together. Marry me, Sammy."

She stared at him for a moment, thinking about it. Finally, she nodded. "All right. I'll marry you."

"Tomorrow?" he pushed.

"You really can't quit while you're ahead, can you?" She bit her lip, thinking. "I do think it would be a good idea for me to wait until after Tabby's baby is born. I'm going to be the only one on call in town for babies for a little while."

"Tomorrow. Before her baby is born. Please don't make me wait."

"You're beginning to remind me of a toddler who *has* to get his own way."

"I'm determined to get my way. Come on. Brother Anthony sounds like he's always ready to perform a wedding."

She finally nodded. "All right. I'll make calls during my lunch tomorrow, but that means you need to bring me food for lunch. I'm not going to be running all over town making calls while I get my taco burger."

"I'll bring you a taco burger and cheese curds."

She used a ladle to put food in two bowls, handing one to him. "I really think this is a weird arrangement, but I'll go with it." She wasn't sure what else to do, and she longed to spend the night in his arms. Surely that meant it would work out between them.

While they ate, she made a list of all the people to call. She decided not to invite either parent. If she invited her dad and Adam, her mother would be uncomfortable around them. If she invited her mother, then her dad and Adam would be angry. No, she'd just get married without either of them. As long as Tabby was there, everything would be just fine.

As soon as she put her pencil down, he took her hand in his. "You've made me the happiest man alive today."

"You've made *me* a nervous wreck. I hope we can meet in the middle somewhere."

He laughed. "I'm sure that's absolutely possible. It'll just take a little time."

"Yeah. Time." She sighed, picking the pencil back up. How could she forget to invite Linda and Roy? The older couple had finally tied the knot, leaving the Culpepper house to Karlan and Hope as they settled into Roy's house in town.

She needed to find a dress, call Brother Anthony—or maybe she'd call Lovee—and figure out flowers and a cake. Thankfully, Grace knew to keep a wedding cake made up at all times. All she had to do was decorate it. It was Culpepper, after all.

*   *   *

The following day was absolutely crazy. Sammy made calls between patients, and again during her lunch. At noon on the dot, Barry showed up with her lunch from Bob's. He had brought a taco burger of his own, and he sat and watched her make phone calls as he ate it. The half of the conversation he heard with Brother Anthony fascinated him more than a little.

"Brother Anthony? I was hoping to get Lovee . . ." Pause. "Yes, I really need you, but she's easier to talk to about these things than you are." Pause. "Yes, that's exactly what I'm going to ask you." Sammy held the phone away from her ear. "Yes, I know it's ridiculous." Pause. "Seven tonight?" Pause. "That sounds great. Thanks, Brother Anthony. Oh, in case you didn't know, this is Sammy Ross." Pause. "See you this evening. Thanks."

He stared at her in confusion. "That was not your typical conversation with a clergyman."

"No, but it was a pretty typical Brother Anthony conversation."

"I really cannot wait to meet this man. It's going to be amazing." She looked at the next person on her list. Dallas. She'd text her instead of calling.

As she worked her way down the list, Barry sat quietly, amazed at all she was able to accomplish with just her phone. So many people were banding together to make their wedding a reality.

"Felicity? May I borrow your wedding dress?" Pause. "Oh, well do you think she'd mind if I borrowed it?" Pause. "Oh, she borrowed it, too? Do you know whose wedding dress it was originally?" Pause. "Great, I'll call her! The wedding is at seven this evening. Bring a covered dish, because . . ."

"There's no time for a caterer!" Then there was hysterical laughter. Barry had to assume it was Felicity on the other end of the line, but the woman sounded positively deranged.

Finally, Sammy shut the ringer on her phone off and tucked the phone back into her pocket. "I have an appointment in five minutes, so I need to get back." She walked him to the door, leaning into him and kissing him. "See you in a few hours. I'll be the one in white. Unless, the dress has been dyed and made into a prom dress, and no one was really sure about that."

He chuckled. "You need to talk to people other than Felicity."

"I know. I like her, but she confuses the snot out of me." She kissed him once more and closed the door right in his face as she ran for the clinic. If she made it through the day, it would be a miracle, and everything would be better. She just knew it.

All of her afternoon patients had already heard when they came in. "Yes, of course you're invited to the wedding," she said over and over to the good ladies of Culpepper. They would have two hundred people there on less than twenty-four–hour notice, and she didn't even care. They were all bringing covered dishes, and that was what really mattered.

Finally, she turned the closed sign on the door and went into her house. The wedding dress had been delivered, as she requested, and she opened the box, saying a silent prayer it wasn't pink. She didn't have time to start calling around for another dress. She'd wear her sister's, but she was pretty sure that had been borrowed as well.

The dress was white. She breathed a sigh of relief as she looked behind her to see Tabby joining her. "I'm here to help the bride get ready for her big day."

"Who has a matron of honor dress for a pregnant woman?" Sammy asked, slightly worried.

"Already taken care of. It's in my old room, and as soon as I get you dressed, I'm going to dress myself." Tabby frowned. "I think you made the right decision not inviting Mom or Dad. They never act right when they're around each other. The divorce may have been amicable, but the past few years have not."

"As long as you're by my side, I think I'll have all the family I'll need."

Thirty minutes later, they were headed to the church. The church lot was full, and they had to park on the street. "You'd think they could leave a spot for the bride and her very pregnant sister," Tabby said with a frown.

"They probably figured we were already there." Sammy lifted the skirt of her wedding gown high to keep it from trailing through a huge snow drift.

"Don't fall! I can't help you up, and there's no way you'd be able to get to your feet in that get up!"

A man who looked vaguely familiar to Sammy stopped beside her and offered his arm. "I would love to escort my future sister-in-law into the church. Then you won't fall."

"Help my sister, too, would you? You've got *two* arms!" She grinned at him as he offered his other arm to Tabby. "It's nice to meet you, Bart. Are you going to move to town and help Barry with the bookstore?"

"I'm considering." He had a gouge above one eye, and his pupils looked a little dilated to Sammy.

"Have you seen a doctor for that concussion yet?" she asked.

He shook his head. "No time."

"I'd like you to meet my sister, Dr. Tabitha O'Donnell. She can look at it before the wedding if you are willing."

He grinned. "I see Barry found the right family to marry into. I'd love it if you'd look at my concussion, Dr. O'Donnell."

Tabby narrowed her eyes. "Did you drive here with a concussion? Do you have a death wish?"

He shrugged. "Not really, but you have to have at least a bit of a death wish to do the rodeo circuit."

"As soon as we get into the church, you're going to sit down and let me look at that. The church has a first aid kit that will have to be good enough for the circumstances."

Bart looked at Sammy. "Is she always this bossy?"

Sammy shrugged. "She's the older sister, and she's a doctor. I think the two things combined mess with her head."

Tabby ignored them as they made their way to the church like some sort of three-headed monster, fighting their way through the snow. As soon as they were inside, Tabby sent Sammy for the first aid kit, and while everyone else watched and waited, Bart was given the most thorough exam possible under the circumstances.

When she was done, Tabby crossed her arms over her chest. "I don't suppose I can talk you into going to the hospital in Laramie."

"I have to be the best man."

Tabby sighed. "And I'm the matron of honor. Walk me down the aisle, so I can watch you and make sure you don't fall over."

"You have the best ideas, doc."

As they walked to the front, Sammy took deep breaths and pretended everyone was seeing her in her wedding gown for the first time instead of watching her play nurse to her sister's doctor for the past ten minutes. She slowly walked down the aisle to the music Lovee was playing on the church's organ.

When she reached the front, Brother Anthony sighed. "You always were one for making grand entrances, Samantha Ross. I remember the time you brought a kitten to church hidden in your dress. No one could figure out why you did such a thing, but you were so proud of yourself. Well, until the kitten got away and jumped from pew to pew, scaring all the old ladies in the whole church."

"Who're you calling an old lady?" Lovee yelled out the question.

"Not you, my beautiful bride!" Brother Anthony cleared his throat. "Dearly beloved, we are gathered here today for another one of those quick weddings this town has become so very fond of. I think it all started the day those Quinlans came into town, and no one was willing to hurt their feelings and do things differently, so it kept—"

"Tony! Back to the service!" Lovee called.

"Oh, that's right." He cleared his throat again. "Dearly beloved, we are gathered here today to join little Samantha Ross and this random bookshop owner whose name I don't know in holy matrimony."

At that, Barry couldn't help it as a loud laugh just boomed out of him. This was the special wedding Sammy had said Brother Anthony would perform? Really? "It's Barry, sir."

"Oh, don't bother telling me. I'll forget again later. I only remember Samantha because I've known her since before she could walk." Brother Anthony shook his head. "Now, marriage is a bond that is meant to join a man and a woman forever. Do you, bookselling man, take Samantha here to be your lawfully wedded wife? To love, honor, and furnish her with books for the rest of her days?"

"I do," Barry answered. He couldn't help but wonder if the marriage could possibly be legal without his name being used, but no one seemed surprised, so this was probably just how he did weddings. He could see Bart laughing like a hyena, and he grinned happily. This was his new reality.

"Do you, Samantha, take this bookman to be your lawfully wedded husband? To love, honor, and make babies with for the rest of your natural life?"

"I sure do, Brother Anthony." Sammy stole a peek at Barry and was thrilled to see how terribly amused he looked. He obviously now understood what was so special about Brother Anthony's weddings.

"Well, then by the power vested in me by God and the glorious state of Wyoming, I do hereby declare you two husband and wife. Go ahead and kiss her, and it'll all be done but the signatures."

Barry turned to Sammy and kissed the giggle right off her lips. "You could have warned me," he whispered.

"Why? It was more fun this way, don't you think?"

He shook his head and turned to face everyone. He glanced over at Bart and saw the butterfly bandages Tabby had used on him. "What's wrong with my brother?"

"Concussion. He didn't have time to see a doctor, so Tabby examined him at the back of the church before the wedding."

"Didn't anyone think that was odd?" he asked.

"People around here are used to Brother Anthony's special weddings. Why would a medical exam phase anyone?"

"Good point." He looked at her in confusion. "Do we walk to the back now?"

"We'll just head over to the fellowship hall and see what food is there. Everyone else will follow us. They know where the food is!"

He shrugged, holding her hand as they walked back down the aisle and toward the fellowship hall. "Is this our reception?"

"Yeah. There won't be any drinking or dancing, but we'll have some time to thank everyone for coming and eat. Cut the cake. All that good stuff."

"Works for me. It's like everyone in town has done a wedding like this before.'

"It seemed like we had them every three weeks like clockwork for a while!" Sammy said, hurrying over to look at the cake. "Grace makes the most amazing cakes. Isn't it beautiful?"

"It sure is. I can't believe she made it so fast."

"I'll teach you more about Culpepper as soon as I have some time. For now, just know she's got lots of experience in shotgun weddings."

Bart joined them then, holding his hand out to shake Barry's. "I found your bride and her sister and assisted them inside, then the sister got all bossy."

Barry grinned. "I see she did a good job on your concussion. Don't ever drive with a concussion again. Better yet, stay here and don't ever get a concussion again. You don't need that rodeo."

"Maybe the rodeo needs me."

"The rodeo will go on with or without you. My bookstore needs you, though . . ."

Bart shook his head. "You just keep trying, big brother."

"Don't worry. I will!"

Chapter 7

Hours later, Samantha grinned at Barry. "I think we can sneak away from this now."

"I was hoping you'd say that soon!" He took her hand and ran from the church, heading straight to his truck. "Is your truck here?"

"No, I rode over with Tabby. I figured we'd want to leave together." She hadn't been sure about taking her car, but it just seemed to make sense.

"You figured right." He got in and drove to her place. "We never talked about where we'd live, but I figured you'd want to stay with the clinic."

"You figured right. Where do you live anyway?" She couldn't believe she'd just married a man, and she had no idea where he lived.

He grinned. "There's a small apartment above the bookstore. Seemed to be the perfect place for me. Of course, now I'll have to rent it out." It wasn't much, but it was a good place for someone who needed a temporary home as he had.

"To Bart?"

"Maybe. What did you think of him?"

"Other than thinking he was reckless to drive with a concussion, I really liked him. He sat quietly while Tabby poked at him, and that's definitely a mark in his favor." She grinned as she remembered how grumpy he'd been while her sister had insisted on bandaging him up.

"I can see where it would be. He loves books as much as I do. Always wanted to be a mystery writer. We used to sit and write together when we were at the same rodeo. We weren't always, but it was nice. We've always been super close."

"Well, then whoever is working can write between customers! Or you can take turns working, and whoever is home can write. It sounds like the perfect situation if the store makes enough." She was very excited at the idea of him making his dream come true by writing a novel.

Barry frowned. "That's the problem. I doubt it will make enough for both of us to survive."

"We can start those advertising things I suggested. The bakery is willing, and so is Bob. I talked to him at the reception."

"Thank you!"

Sammy shrugged. "I'm happy to help where I can. I also have an in with the girl who does the radio ads. I could talk to her and see if she'd cut you a break, and we could plan a grand opening kind of thing."

"Who does the radio ads?"

"She just moved to town a few months ago, but I really like her. Her name is Courtney Raymond. I met her when her sister, who already lived here, had a baby. Then she moved to town a few months later. She's pretty awesome." Sammy vaguely wondered how Courtney and Bart would like each other, but she didn't say anything.

"Cool." He stopped the truck in front of the clinic. "We're finally alone." He gave her his best lecherous look, and she giggled.

"And I didn't even have to cook!" she said enthusiastically. "That's the best part about it being *my* wedding. No cooking necessary!"

He laughed. "Well, I cook some, too. We won't only have a choice of Bob's burgers or your cooking. I promise."

"Glad to hear it. I do get called away more than I would like. Babies like to be born at night."

"I've heard that!" Barry said. "We'll make it work." He grabbed his suitcase from behind the seat in his truck. "I just brought enough clothes for a couple of days. I figure I'll move in slowly. I don't have a renter for the apartment yet anyway."

"Is that where Bart's staying while he's in town?"

"Yeah. He's been told not to drive for a week. The concussion is worse than he realized." Barry shook his head about his brother driving with a concussion.

"Tabby was appalled. And we had him help us into the church, and halfway in I noticed the mark above his head and his dilated pupils. She dealt with him, but she was annoyed we'd had him help."

"It wasn't her fault. It was his. And with a head as thick as my brother's I'm surprised he was able to get a concussion."

"Does he get them often?"

Barry shrugged. "It goes with being on the circuit. I've had at least a dozen." He tried to play off the multiple injuries he'd dealt with, even as he worried about his brother going down the same road he had.

"I can't believe you say that so casually, and I'm thrilled you're not doing that anymore."

"Me too. Mostly."

Sammy frowned at him as she set her purse onto the couch. "What do you mean mostly? Do you miss it?" She suddenly could picture herself with two kids, at home alone, while he was off riding a bronco. It was not a life she wanted for herself or her future children—imaginary or not.

"Sometimes. It was such a big part of my life for so long. I know I made the right decision when I stopped, but that doesn't mean I don't miss my friends and the crowds."

"Would you ever go back?"

He shook his head. "No. It wouldn't make sense for me to go back. I'd injure myself again, and it would be all over. If the bookstore doesn't pan out and I can't make enough money from writing, I'll find someone around town looking for a hired hand. I'm pretty darn good with horses and cows."

"I'm sure you are. You couldn't help but be good with them."

"I keep telling Bart the same thing. We talked for a bit at the reception, and I told him to work for me part time and find a part-time job as a cow hand. Wouldn't be nearly as dangerous as staying on the circuit, and we'd be close."

"Does he have a relationship with his father?" Sammy asked.

Barry nodded. "He does. His dad wouldn't back off when Mom tried to force him to stop seeing Bart. My brother spent every summer with his dad, and I was always so jealous of him for getting to do that."

"I can see that. You didn't have a dad, and you thought of his father as a dad . . . you would have had to be very jealous. How long was his dad married to your mom?"

"Three years, I think. Probably her longest marriage if I think about it." He frowned. "No, that was Bob. She was married to Bob for six years or so. The whole time I was in high school, and a couple of years more."

"Was Bob a good man?"

He shrugged. "Sure. He had a ranch, and I got to learn a lot. I didn't mind him."

Sammy was a little surprised at how little she knew about this man she'd married. Of course, they'd known one another less than a week. What had she been thinking?

He kissed her then, and she remembered exactly what she'd been thinking. She'd been thinking he turned her insides to mush every time he got close to her.

She moved closer to him, wrapping her arms around him, thrilled that this time, they wouldn't have to stop. She felt his hands on the little buttons on the back of her dress, and she pushed his jacket off his shoulders.

Her dress was pooled at her feet when she heard an incessant beeping. She tore away from him. "I have to see who's texting."

"Ignore it!" He reached for her again, pulling her back toward him.

"I can't. It might be a patient." As much as she wanted to ignore it, there was no way she could.

He groaned softly but allowed her to move away from him.

She apologized as she read the message. "I'm so sorry. With my work, I don't have a choice but to be chained to messages." She read through it. "I have a patient on her way. She'll be at the clinic in five.

Baby's on the way." She hurried to him, kissing him softly. "Changing into my scrubs, and I'll be back when I can."

He nodded, watching her run off. He wondered how much of his married life would be this way.

* * *

Sammy crawled into bed at just after seven the following morning. "I'm going to get thirty minutes sleep before I have to start my day. I will probably nap through my lunch hour."

"I can bring you a burger." Barry propped up on one elbow, looking down at his beautifully exhausted wife.

She shook her head. "I'll be too tired to eat. I keep little snacks at the office, and I'll eat them between patients. I'll be fine." With those words, her eyes were closed, and she was sound asleep.

He watched her for a moment before getting out of bed. Hopefully she would get enough sleep and not be exhausted all day. He wanted to make love with her but not to her detriment. She needed her sleep.

Sammy was dragging all day. She was thankful for the nuts and raisin snacks she had hidden in a variety of places around the office. They would keep her going between naps. She had an hour and a half break in the morning between patients, and she took it in her bed, getting up just in time to meet with her next patient.

As she'd told Barry she would, she slept through her lunch hour. By the time she got off work, she was ready to climb into bed for the rest of her life. She was sleeping before Barry got home, and he quietly made supper, waking her up to eat it. "I know how tired you are, but you need to eat as well."

She nodded, her eyes mostly closed as she ate the omelet he'd made. "I'm sorry. I want to spend time with you, but I need to sleep!"

He nodded. "I know. By midnight, you'll feel like you again, and we'll spend some time together then."

She smiled, wiping her mouth. "Midnight sounds lovely." She walked back into the bedroom and was asleep as soon as her head hit the pillow.

At eleven thirty, he showered and got ready for bed, knowing she'd finally have a little more energy and they could pick up where they left off. Just as he walked into the bedroom, her text notification went off again. She sat up, reaching for her phone.

Whatever she read made her jump to attention. "Tabby's in labor. I have just enough time to shower before she gets here. I'm going to be an aunt!"

Barry sat down on his side of the bed. "Congratulations." Obviously, he'd be waiting a while before anything happened with his new wife, but that was all right. She was going to be an aunt.

He climbed into bed and laid on his back, staring at the ceiling. He knew she had to do her job, but he was ready to have a real marriage as well. He closed his eyes, reminding himself that this is what he'd signed up for. She'd told him a few times that emergencies had to come first. This was an emergency. All births were.

Sammy delivered her nephew around noon the following day and carefully put him into Dallas's arms. "I can't believe you called a sub just so you could help me with this delivery."

"I can't believe you'd be surprised," Dallas returned with a smile. She carefully bathed the baby before laying him in Tabby's arms.

"I don't even know what you're naming him!" Sammy said. How had her sister never divulged that information?

Tabby sighed. "We've been arguing about his name since we found out it was a boy. You'll know as soon as a real decision has been made."

"All right. But my nephew cannot be nameless forever!"

"He won't be. I hope."

Sammy washed her hands and cleaned up the room. "I can't believe Arch isn't here!"

"He took that business trip, knowing I wasn't due for two more weeks. I called him, and he headed back, but . . . he didn't make it in time."

"Well, you did great. I'm excited for you." Sammy kissed her sister's cheek. "I had Angela call everyone to cancel all appointments for today. So, I'm going to get a nap before my husband gets home. You okay?"

Tabby nodded. "I'm going to stay here for another hour or two. I know what to do."

"I know you do. I wouldn't leave anyone else this way." Sammy left the clinic and went back to her house, leaving Dallas in charge. She stripped and climbed into bed, hoping for a few hours of sleep before Barry got home.

* * *

Barry left work on Wednesday afternoon and went up to his apartment to get more clothes. He couldn't believe he'd been married forty-eight hours and he still hadn't made love with his new wife. Hopefully the run of deliveries would cool off for long enough for them to consummate the marriage before she had to run off again.

Bart was there, still hurting and sleeping most of the time.

"You made any decisions yet?" Barry asked.

Bart shook his head. "No, but I'm thinking seriously about your offer. If I could find a part-time job helping out on a ranch, I could spend the rest of the time at the bookstore with you, and we could take turns getting our books written."

"I can give you the names of a few men in the area who might be hiring. I think Sammy would be able to expand on the list if you're really interested."

Bart frowned. "Do you miss the rodeo?"

"Honestly, I do sometimes, but I'm glad I left. It was breaking me physically. There's no crowd that can cheer loud enough to make that worth it. And I have my bookstore, and now I'm married to Sammy . . .

no I made the best decision for me. I can't make your decision for you, though if I could, I'd tell you to leave. You don't need to ruin your life with injuries."

Bart nodded. "I'll consider. I've thought of nothing else during my waking moments since I got here."

"Well, you probably need to recover from that concussion before you worry about it too terribly much."

"I agree with that." Bart shook his head. "I love my life, but I'll love it more if I'm not constantly worried about dying."

"Good." Barry got to his feet, his packed bag beside him. "Anything you need before I head back? I could run to the store for you."

Bart sighed. "What I really want is a burger. Are there any good burgers in town? I don't think I could stay on my feet long enough to cook one."

"I can get you one from next door. There's a place called Bob's Burger Barn. I swear Bob is a genius. Best burgers I've ever had, hands down." Barry frowned at his brother. "I'll get you one before I head back."

Bart shook his head. "If it's next door, there's no driving involved, and I think the fresh air would do me good. I'll head over myself."

"I'll walk over with you, just to make sure you're steady on your feet."

Bart shrugged. "You don't have to, but I'd enjoy the company. Give me five minutes."

As they walked, Barry told Bart about all the different burgers available. Bob was still there when they walked in. Bob usually only worked during the day. "Bob, this is my brother Bart. He's craving a burger."

Bob grinned. "You came to the right place."

Barry ordered a couple of taco burgers to go and sat with his brother while they were cooked. "You have to try the fried cheese curds," Barry told Bart. "They're amazing."

"I don't even know what that is!"

"It doesn't matter. You just have to try it!"

"Fine, I'll try it!" Bart shrugged. "Everything on this menu looks amazing."

Barry grinned. "Well, if you don't mind working with the cows after they're dead, you should get a job as a cook from Bob. He is hiring right now, and you're an excellent cook."

Bart frowned. "Cooking in a restaurant? I don't know about that . . ."

"Just until your first book sells."

"I'll think on it."

Bob came then with Barry's to-go order and took Bart's order. Barry slipped out of the booth. "See you soon."

"I may wander down to the bookstore tomorrow. I'm staying awake a little longer at a time as the concussion heals."

"Sounds good." Barry left, heading to his truck. He wanted to get home with the burgers before Sammy started supper.

When he got home, he found his wife in a pair of old pajamas, looking exhausted. She was standing in the middle of the kitchen, looking around as if she was confused.

"What are you doing?" he asked.

"Trying to figure out what to make for supper. I'm so tired!"

He smiled, holding up the bag in his hand. "I stopped at Bob's."

Sammy was ready to cry with relief. "And this is why I married you!" She took the bag from his hand, grabbed a couple of plates, and took it to the table. "How was work?"

"Great. I had my best sales day yet. The bakery didn't wait for a flyer and has been talking me up to locals and visitors."

"Oh, good. I was hoping they'd start on that soon." She pulled her burger from the bag and put the cheese curds in the middle of the table. "How's Bart doing?"

"That's why I went to Bob's. He wanted a burger, so I walked him over. He was pretty amazed at all the different kinds of burgers Bob had available." He took one of the cheese curds and popped it into his mouth. "Tabby's baby is okay?"

She nodded, her eyes lit up. "I deliver babies all the time. Not every day, but several a month. And I have to say, there is nothing like delivering a baby that's related to you. I held that little boy and just cried."

"I'm glad! What did they name him?"

Sammy shrugged. "They hadn't picked out a name yet. I'm sure they'll let me know soon, though, because I have to put it on the birth certificate."

"Sounds good to me." He reached out and took her hand in his. "I've hated having to sleep without you the past couple of nights."

She sighed. "I'm sorry I keep running off. I'm going to be delivering double the number of babies now, too, with Tabby being on maternity leave." She shook her head. "That's why I suggested waiting to get married until she was back."

"I'm glad we didn't wait, but I wish you were home a little more."

"Me too!" She finished her meal and leaned back. "I'm going to take a shower and get ready for bed. I know it's early, but my sleep has been messed up by all the babies being delivered."

"I'll be waiting for you," he said, winking at her.

"I appreciate the waiting." As she walked past him, Sammy kissed his forehead. She did hate that she was called away just when things were getting all hot and heavy between them. At least they hadn't had a chance to get started the night before.

After her shower, she walked into the bedroom, and he was sitting on the side of the bed, frowning.

"What's wrong?" she asked.

"You got a text."

She groaned. "Are you kidding? This town needs to stop having babies already!"

He grinned. "At least I know it bugs you as much as it does me."

She took her phone and glanced at the screen. "They're going to be at the clinic in five minutes. I need to change into scrubs." She looked down at the frilly nightgown she was wearing. "I tried."

"I know you did. It'll happen. There aren't enough people in this town to have babies every night forever."

"This is true. The full moon will be over in a couple of days. It always slows down after that."

Barry grinned. "I thought someone just made that up!" Full moons really had an impact on the number of babies born?

"No, there really are more babies born during a full moon. It's nutty." She grabbed her scrubs and hurried into the bathroom to change. When she was finished, she went back into the bedroom and kissed hm. "See you after this baby is born."

"It's a good thing you love what you do so much."

"Isn't it?" she asked. She ran from the room, because she was too tempted to stay with him and make a baby of their own. Her hours had never bothered her before, and now they were getting on her last nerve.

She hurried to the clinic and got things ready for the delivery, realizing how much she missed her sister as part of this process. They usually did everything side by side.

While she waited for her patient, she called Tabby. "What's my nephew's name?"

Tabby laughed. "I think we're naming him Wright. Arch is a big fan of Frank Lloyd Wright, so we're naming him Wright Steven. I wanted to name him Steven."

"Works for me! I'll put it on his birth certificate. How are you feeling?"

"Tired, but good. No problems. If there are any, you know I'll call."

"Good." Sammy heard the front door. "My next delivery is here. Talk to you soon!"

"Let me know if you need me!"

"Don't worry. Even with you delivering today, I won't risk a baby for lack of help." There was a doctor in Haskell they could call as well, but Tabby was closer for emergencies. Sammy certainly would choose the right person to call if it came to that. "Love you!"

"Love you, too!"

Chapter 8

Sammy got home after eight the next morning. Barry was waiting for her. "You all right?"

She nodded. "I'm having my secretary reschedule morning appointments. I'll go in at one." She was weaving on her feet. She needed sleep more than she needed anything else at that moment.

He shook his head. "I don't know how you're able to keep going with all this."

"I have no choice. When Tabby is working as well, we handle things better because we work so closely together. But she's out, too, so I'm going to have to handle it."

"I'm worried about you. You look exhausted."

She nodded. "I am. I'm going to grab a bowl of cereal and head back to bed. I'll get up in time for a shower and lunch and see afternoon patients."

"How can I help?" he asked, willing to do anything to take the fatigued look from her eyes.

"Bring me lunch at noon. I'll eat, shower, and work. But I won't have to cook for myself, and today, I don't know if I can handle cooking for myself or anyone else."

"Will do." He leaned down and kissed her. "I'm heading to work. I will see you at noon with burgers."

She nodded, getting herself a bowl of cereal and plopping down at the table to eat it. She rubbed her hands over her face, thankful there had been no complications in the past three deliveries. It always scared her a little to work without Tabby to back her up. Sure, she knew *how* to perform an emergency c-section, because she had assisted Tabby multiple times, but having a real live obstetrician ready to back her up was a safety net she didn't like to work without.

Fifteen minutes later, she was sound asleep after a quick prayer for no deliveries for a day or two. She wasn't sure she could handle more.

* * *

Barry had his best sales day ever. People had realized he was in town before he'd married Sammy, but it seemed after going to his wedding and getting to know him a bit, a lot more people were willing to shop in his store. There was definitely a mentality of only wanting to buy from people who were familiar in the town.

It was halfway through the morning when Bart came into the store, taking a seat beside his brother behind the desk. Barry finished ringing up his customer and turned to his brother. "Sales are really picking up."

Bart grinned. "That's wonderful. I am really happy for you."

"But not for you?" Barry asked, a frown on his face.

"Well, for me, too. I talked to Bob for a while yesterday, and as soon as I'm cleared to work, I have a job in his kitchen. He'll let me work starting at six in the evening until ten at night, so I can work in the bookstore until it closes."

Barry wanted to jump to his feet and pump his fist, but he knew his brother wouldn't be pleased with him for it. "Any idea when you're going to be cleared to work?"

Bart shrugged. "This was my worst concussion yet. My mind is going to be Jell-O before too terribly long if I keep at it in the rodeo, so this is the best solution. Tabby thinks I should go to the hospital in Laramie to be checked out. She said she's not used to working with concussions."

"Then I'd go to Laramie. Do you need me to drive you?"

"Maybe tomorrow? That way you can have a sign in your door all day saying that you're going to be gone. I'd hate for you to miss a ton of business because of me."

"I appreciate that, but your health comes first," Barry said. "I need to head home at lunch today to take lunch to Sammy. She's had deliveries the past three nights, and she looks like she's about to fall over."

"What a way to honeymoon!" Bart said, shaking his head. "It must be fun to be married to a woman who knows so much about babies though, huh?"

Barry shook his head. "I wish she was a secretary or something. Then she wouldn't always look like she was about to pass out. Oh, Tabby was one of those deliveries. She had a healthy boy."

Bart smiled. "That's awesome. Your wife is a superhero. She makes babies magically appear!"

"Yes, she does. She's good at it, too."

"Well, I'm going to go up to your apartment and go back to bed."

Barry shook his head. "Your apartment. I'll have the rest of my stuff cleared out this weekend. We'll figure out rent later. Or I can take it out of your paycheck. Whatever you want."

"Works for me." Bart walked toward the door. "See you tomorrow. We should probably go in the morning."

"Sounds good." Barry would have taken Bart at any time, and he was thrilled his brother had finally agreed to go to the hospital. Hopefully he wouldn't need to be admitted to the hospital and would just be given instructions on what to do.

After he'd gone, Barry pulled up his book on his computer. It was his first chance to write since the wedding, and he was going to take advantage of it. He needed to start taking his book home with him at night for evenings when Sammy was out delivering, but he hadn't started yet.

He didn't want to have to take it back and forth on a flash drive, so he did some quick research and chose a service where he could save the book onto an internet drive. That way he could write no matter what his location was.

He glanced up when the bell over the door rang and smiled as Grace, Patience, and Felicity all came in. He had met all three of them at the reception, and he knew they ran the bakery in town. "How can I help you ladies?"

"We're just looking for books," Felicity said. "I sure hope you're treating my favorite midwife well, because she's amazing and deserves to be treated like a princess, and if you don't treat her like a princess, I might have to gather a posse to come after you and cut your toes off one by one."

Barry blinked. Was that all one sentence? It had sure sounded like one. "I'm barely seeing her at the moment. She keeps getting called out to deliver babies." He wasn't worried that the woman would get to his toes. Besides, he treated his wife as a man should.

Grace walked in front of her cousin. "I heard Tabby had her baby and it went well. We're all excited to see him."

Patience nodded, moving next to Grace and turning her back on her sister, who had apparently lost her mind . . . again. "I'm sure it's hard on Sammy right now with Tabby out of the picture. Tell her if there's anything non-medical people can do, we'll be there."

"I'll tell her. Thank you." Barry was glad that the other two women weren't quite as bizarre as Felicity. "What kind of books are you looking for?"

"Romance," Grace said. "The kind of stuff we weren't allowed to read when we were younger because our parents were insane. You got anything good?"

He laughed softly. "I will take you to the romance section. Sammy told me it needs help, and she's going to help me reorganize it as soon as she has time." He led the three women to the romances, noting that Felicity looked bigger than Tabby had. "When are you due?"

"Three more months." Felicity turned to the side to show off her huge tummy. "I'm going to pop, huh!"

He looked noticeably shocked. "Umm . . . are you supposed to be that big?"

Patience and Grace both started laughing. "She's having twins," Patience explained.

"Oh! I thought she was going to have the first thirty-pound baby!"

Felicity shook her head. "Nope. My first was eight pounds. I don't want these two to get any bigger than that!"

Barry decided not to say anything else on the subject. He was not an expert on pregnancies even though he was married to a midwife. "I'll let you ladies browse. Let me know if you need anything."

"Just those flyers we've been promised," Grace said.

"I'll have them to you by Monday, I hope." He looked at the three of them for a moment. "Who's watching the bakery?"

"Rikki, our employee. We just took off for an hour so we could come check out the store. We'll all work an hour late to make up for it," Patience said.

"Ahh, then I'll get out of your way so you can use your time off wisely." He walked back to his computer, thinking he could write a paragraph or two.

As soon as he was sitting down, more customers came into the store. He was seriously surprised by the sheer number of people who were coming in this week as opposed to last week. Business was definitely improving.

* * *

At lunchtime, Barry picked up two burgers, taking one home to Sammy. He woke her, and she moved to the table, yawning behind her hand. "I wish this wasn't so hard on you!"

"It goes with the job. Not a big deal." She reached for her burger and smiled. "Thank you for bringing lunch."

"Are you still going in this afternoon?" he asked. He wanted to add up the number of hours she'd slept, but he was afraid to.

"I need to. We rescheduled a lot of people, but there are a few patients we just can't put off. Don't worry. I've done this before, and I'm not dead!"

"I can see you're not dead, and I'm glad. But are you sure you're not hurting yourself by doing so much?"

She shrugged. "I won't do any permanent damage. I promise."

"I saw Felicity today. Is she really only six months?"

Sammy grinned and nodded. "She's having twins, and she carries high, which makes her look huge."

"Well, I was worried she was having a thirty-pound baby."

"Nope, should be two seven or eight pound babies. She's super healthy and doing great. I told her to lay off her own cookies for a bit or she'd gain too much, but she seems to have done so. It's so hard for any woman to do well keeping her weight down while pregnant."

"I wasn't trying to comment on her weight. Do you think I offended her?"

Sammy shook her head. "It takes more than that to offend Felicity. The girl is crazily awesome."

"She threatened to cut my toes off if I'm not kind to you."

Sammy laughed. "Sounds like Felicity. Once she likes someone, they are her person forever. She would protect me from anyone or anything, whether she had the chance of being injured or not. Wait until you try her cookies. They're like little pieces of heaven baked into a cookie."

"I might have to stop there and buy some. They sound fabulous. Do you have a favorite kind?"

She shook her head. "Not at all, but it doesn't matter because I love them all."

He got to his feet. "I need to get back to the shop. I'm going to close tomorrow and take Bart to Laramie to get his head examined." He laughed at his own joke.

She shook her head. "Let me know what the doctor says."

"Oh! And he's going to work for me part time and for Bob part time. He's staying."

Sammy jumped to her feet and threw her arms around him. "I'm so happy he's staying."

Barry kissed her. "I sure wish I had more time with you, because I want a real marriage, but hopefully tonight will be our night."

She smiled. "I think I could find energy for that . . . if I got another nap."

"I'll plan on making supper, then. Don't expect anything fancy, but I'll cook while you nap."

"You're the best husband I've ever had!"

"Umm . . . you've been married before?"

"Not unless you count the boy I married in high school. It was a mock wedding, and my dress was beautiful . . ."

"No, I don't count that. Not one little bit."

"Oh, then you're the only husband I've ever had."

He kissed her softly. "Have a good afternoon." And then he'd disappeared out the door. She was going to miss him.

She hurried off to their bedroom to change into scrubs while saying a silent prayer there would be no more deliveries that day. Or the next. Two days straight would be good. She loved what she did, but she needed sleep and some private time with her new husband. Was that too much to ask?

When she got to the clinic, her first patient was waiting. "How are you feeling, Hope?"

Hope shrugged. "This is my second pregnancy, and everything seems to be just fine. Do I really need to come in every month?"

"I think it's best if you do." As Sammy examined Hope Culpepper, she couldn't help but wonder what the other woman thought of her cousin, Felicity, who was proving to be bigger than a house.

"All right. I just hate leaving Linda with all the little ones." Hope yawned. "I do wish there was more time to sleep."

"Me too!"

Hope grinned. "I've heard the full moon brought you a run on babies."

"So many babies! And without Tabby to help."

"How's Tabby doing? Have they named the baby yet?"

"They're calling him Wright after Frank Lloyd Wright. Seems a little odd to me, but that's Arch and Tabby for you. Their entire courtship was one practical joke after another."

"That's true . . ." Hope shook her head. "Felicity is so proud of how huge she looks. Is she wearing any kind of padding to look bigger?"

Sammy laughed. "I don't think she needs padding. That woman is *all* baby!"

"She seriously looks like she's about to explode. Baby and guts everywhere."

"I promise, she's not exploding yet. She's just big. Twins do that to a woman."

"Well, her baby bump is more of a baby mountain, and she has months to go yet!"

"Yup. She's going to be just fine, though, and no, there's no padding at all." Sammy looked at Hope. "You're sixteen weeks. Do you want to take a peek and see what sex the baby is?"

"I thought we couldn't do that until twenty weeks." Hope suddenly looked a great deal more awake, and she nodded emphatically. "Karlan keeps telling me that he's only going to be fathering boys, and since the first was a boy, I have to prove him wrong. I want a girl. Can you spritz some girl mojo onto the wand?"

"Absolutely! Lay back, and we'll make this happen!" One of Sammy's favorite parts of her job was doing sonograms and letting people know if they were having a boy or a girl. "I'm putting all the girl juju into this that I can!"

"You're the best!" Hope said, lying on her back and straining to see the monitor.

Sammy went over different things, pointing out arms, legs, head . . . "I'm not seeing what I would need to see for it to be a boy, so that leaves me only one possible conclusion!"

"A girl! I'm so excited! In your *face,* Karlan Culpepper!"

"I'm not sure that helping you fight with your husband over the baby's gender is part of my job description."

"Would you print out a view of between the legs with no tail, please? I can't wait to show him!"

Sammy laughed softly at the request, but she immediately did it, handing the printout to Hope after helping her sit up. "Now you have proof that there's a girl on the way. Linda is going to be so happy!"

"I know! I mean, she loves little boys, but she loves little girls, too. She is going to have a whole room full of Barbies, and she's the kind of grandma who will get down on the floor with them. Roy isn't going to know what hit him!" Hope shook her head. "I'm so excited!"

"Well, I can't wait to hear what Karlan says. Will you text me after you've told him?"

"Yes!" Hope giggled. "I'll probably take out a skywriter."

"Well, if you take out a skywriter, then text me before it flies over. I need to see his reaction!"

"Oh, the whole world is going to know his reaction." Hope got to her feet and hugged Sammy. "I'm so glad we peeked!"

"Me too!" Sammy watched as Hope hurried out of the office, thrilled with her reaction to finding out it was a girl. Experiences like that made all of the sleepless nights worth it.

The rest of the afternoon flew by, and she finally went home, sagging onto the couch. She was so tired, but she was determined to stay awake and enjoy her evening with her new husband. Could she even call him a husband yet since they hadn't done each other? She had no idea, but what else was she going to call him?

She heard the door open, and Barry came in. "I'm making nachos. I hope you like jalapenos."

"Love 'em! I'm just going to sit here and nap while you cook, unless you need me."

"Oh, I need you, but not to help me make nachos. Sleep! I want you rested for later."

Sammy closed her eyes and drifted off to sleep, ignoring the sounds of him in the kitchen cooking. As long as she didn't have to cook, she would be one happy wife.

Chapter 9

Sammy woke up with Barry leaning over her. "Time to eat. I hope you're hungry."

She sat up and wiped her eyes. "Sure. Hungry."

He shook his head. "You're more tired than hungry. You really wipe yourself out, don't you?"

She shrugged. "Comes with the job."

"Come eat." He led her to the table. "My famous nachos."

She looked at the table. He'd browned meat and added refried beans and cheese. There were chips, and she could see tiny pieces of chopped up jalapenos. It looked good. "I can see why they're famous." She sat down.

"Do you want a Sprite? Or something else?"

"Sprite sounds good." She yawned. "And water. Get me both."

"You're being a little high maintenance."

"I'm sorry." But she didn't change what she wanted to just one. She wanted the Sprite, but she knew she needed the water. On days when she was going too much, she rarely got enough to stay properly hydrated.

Barry came back to the table with the drinks she'd asked for and a root beer for himself. He sat across from her and nodded to her nachos. "How do you like them?"

"I was waiting to try them until you came back to the table. I didn't want to be rude." She'd been tempted, though. They did look good!

"Try one!" He shook his head, like she'd lost her mind.

"They're good!" She opened her Sprite and took a sip. "Thank you for cooking."

"I'm not sure you can count nachos as cooking."

"It's more than I could have done tonight."

He told her about Bart deciding to stay in town as they ate.

"Does this mean we get a discount from Bob's?"

Barry laughed. "No, but Bob will put a flyer in every to-go order and have one on every table."

"That's probably better than a discount! Awesome!" Sammy kept eating her nachos. They really were good and not what she'd expected at all. She thought he'd just throw some cheese on chips and microwave them. This was infinitely better.

After they'd finished eating, he sent her back to the couch. "Sleep for a few more minutes while I get the dishes washed."

"You're doing dishes, too? I think you must be the most wonderful man ever." She kissed him quickly before doing as he'd told her and lying back down on the couch. Every minute of sleep she got at that moment was absolutely precious.

When Barry finished with the dishes, he sat beside her, determined to let her sleep for another hour or so. She was curled into a little ball on her side, so there was plenty of room for him. He grabbed her remote and turned on the show he'd been binge watching, making sure the volume was low.

It was two hours later when she woke up and looked at him. "I really did crash, didn't I?"

He nodded. "But you needed sleep. All is good." He paused the show he was watching and turned to her. "Feeling better?"

She nodded emphatically. "Yes!"

"Good. Because I have plans for the rest of your evening."

She grinned, sitting up and moving toward him. "Tell me about these plans."

He wrapped his arm around her and brought her lips to his. "I thought we could start with a little kissing . . ."

"Oh! I like kissing."

They sat together on the couch for twenty minutes, gently exploring one another as they kissed. It was leisurely, not as intense as usual. It was obvious Barry was half-expecting to be interrupted at any moment, and he wasn't putting his heart into it.

"Do you think maybe it's time to move this party to the bedroom?" she asked softly.

"Sounds great to me!" He grabbed her hand and tugged her toward the bedroom. "Maybe you should put your phone on mute." He was joking but only sort of. He was determined that someone was watching and deliberately going into labor as soon as they started trying to husband and wife.

She frowned. "You know I can't do that."

"I do. I wish you could, but I understand." He pushed her down onto the bed and followed her down, kissing her madly, finally amping up the passion. Now that they'd actually made it to the bed, he was feeling optimistic that this would be able to make it to its natural conclusions.

She was still wearing her scrubs from work, and he pulled her shirt off, silently thinking this was the furthest they'd ever gotten. It was probably time for the text. When there was no sound, he cupped her breasts in his hands, his thumbs finding her nipples through the sheer silkiness of her bra.

When she moaned, he knew she was with him, and he rained kisses over the tops of her breasts that were visible through the bra before reaching behind her, unclasping it, and throwing it to the floor. For a moment, he just stared at what he'd uncovered before leaning down and taking one nipple into his mouth and sucking on it softly, his tongue toying with the tip.

He stood up then and stripped off his own clothes, leaning down and divesting her of her scrub bottoms and panties.

Covering her with his body again, he moved his hands all over her body. "You all right?" he asked softly.

She nodded. "So good!"

And that's when the sound came. He groaned and rolled to his back. "I swear I'm going to kill that thing one of these days."

She reached for her phone and read the text message. *Karlan didn't believe me at first, and then he looked at the part of the sonogram you'd circled for him. He thinks you did it deliberately through some kind of sorcery.*

Sammy laughed and looked over at Barry, who was lying on his back with his arm thrown over his eyes, obviously frustrated. She moved over to him, and started kissing him.

After a moment, he pulled away. "Not a delivery?"

"Just a patient letting me know her husband's reaction to having a little girl instead of a boy."

"Does that mean we can finally finish what we started?"

"Unless I get another text . . ."

He shook his head, laughing softly. "It's laugh or cry at this point."

"I'd prefer to skip both and just make love."

"I can do that, too . . ."

* * *

Afterward, Sammy lay on her side, her head pillowed on Barry's shoulder. "We didn't get interrupted," she said softly.

He chuckled. "I wasn't sure we'd ever make it through." Kissing her forehead, he added, "The wait was so worth it."

"Well, I'm glad to hear it!" She snuggled closer. "I think I'm going to like being married."

"I know I will." He gathered her even closer, holding her. "Maybe our rotten streak is broken now, and we won't get interrupted every time we start kissing."

"I sure hope so. And speaking of interruptions . . . I'm going to need to text Hope back."

"She's the one who texted you and almost made me die of anguish?"

"Feeling a little dramatic this evening?" she asked.

He shook his head. "Not at all. Feeling a little . . . satisfied."

"Glad to hear it!" She reached for her phone and quickly tapped out a response. *Tell Karlan the gender is determined by the man.*

"Now I have the munchies," he said.

"The munchies? What are you hungry for?"

"No idea." He got out of bed. "I'm going to go see what I can scrounge. You hungry?"

She shook her head. "Not at all. Just tired. I think I'm going to shower really quick and sleep."

He looked at his phone. "It's only eight-thirty."

"I know, but if there are no deliveries tonight, I'm going to be well-rested tomorrow."

"A well-rested wife sounds good to me." He wandered out of the bedroom in search of food, while she headed for the bathroom and her shower.

* * *

Saturday morning, Sammy went to visit her new nephew while Barry went to the store. When she got to Tabby's house, she was greeted by a very harried Arch. "The baby wants nothing to do with me. He just wants to eat and sleep!"

"That's pretty normal," Sammy told him. "He doesn't need anyone but Mama for the first few months, and then Daddy becomes important."

Arch frowned. "But I want to be important now! Do you think he's mad at me for not being there when he was born?"

Sammy just laughed. "Where are they?"

"In the living room. He's nursing, and she's smiling contentedly."

Sammy headed to the living room and found her sister and nephew exactly as Arch had said she would. "Good morning."

Tabby looked up with a grin on her face. "Good morning. I have a baby."

Sammy sat down beside her sister on the couch. "How's he nursing?" she asked.

"Beautifully. I was sure I was going to have to come to you for lactation help, but he's doing great." Sammy was a midwife and a lactation consultant, and she was proud to do both jobs. Most of the time, midwifery had to come first, though.

"I'm so glad he's doing so well." Sammy's arms ached to hold him, but he was nursing so well, she didn't dare even suggest it.

"Arch was mortified he missed the birth. He's convinced the baby is mad at him for not being there for it." Tabby giggled. "I may have told him he'd have to do something to make it up to both of us."

"You're mean!" Sammy said, grinning. "He tried so hard to get here on time."

"I know he did, but he shouldn't have gone on that business trip."

"Did you tell him that before he left? Or did you wait until he'd missed the birth to start giving him advice about when to travel?" Sammy knew her sister and how she was. She had a feeling about what the answer would be.

"Well, not until he got home, but he should have known not to travel." Tabby looked down at the baby again. "His little cheeks are so soft. With all the babies I've delivered, you'd think he wouldn't be quite so amazing to me."

"Well, you did make and cook this one yourself."

Little Wright finally stopped nursing, and Tabby offered him to Sammy. "He's all yours if you want him."

Sammy took him eagerly. "How could you tell I was dying to play auntie and hold my nephew?"

"It was written all over your face. I'm glad you're as excited as I am about him."

"There's no doubt. I'm glad one of us finally had a baby!"

"You're up next. You two trying?" Tabby asked.

Sammy nodded. "I want a couple of babies, and I don't think I should wait much longer if I want them to be healthy." They both knew the risks of having a baby when you were over thirty-five.

"I'm sure you won't have any issues. And you know I'll help you out if you do."

Sammy wrinkled her nose. She didn't want to have to take drugs that would put her at risk for multiples. "I know. Thank you!"

"How's married life?"

"Good! Barry is absolutely amazing!"

Tabby smiled. "You'll have to bring me some books from his store. You know what I like." She reached to her side and picked her purse up off the floor, pulling out fifty dollars. "I'm going to have a little time to read while I'm home with him."

"I'm happy to do it." Sammy tucked the money into her pocket, careful not to dislodge the baby.

"Any deliveries this week? Other than mine of course?"

Sammy laughed. "Three total. Every time Barry even thought of getting amorous, I'd get a text for another delivery."

Tabby laughed. "That's how it goes, doesn't it?"

"But all babies were born happy and healthy." Sammy listed the other two mothers who had given birth during the week.

"Well, hopefully that won't *always* happen, but it will continue to happen. The whole situation has frustrated Arch more than once."

"It's what they signed on for when they married us," Sammy said with a shrug. "I warned Barry, and I'm sure . . . well, you didn't get a chance to warn Arch, did you?"

"I still can't believe all of you tricked me into marrying him."

"Well, you would never have gotten there on your own. You two were flirting *forever*."

Tabby just shook her head, refusing to talk about it more.

Arch came into the room then, frowning at Sammy. "How come he lets Sammy hold him and not me?"

"Sammy was there when he was born. She caught him coming out, like you were supposed to." Tabby smiled sweetly at Arch, but it was obvious she wasn't going to let it go for a while. Sammy hoped that she and Barry never got to that point, but she'd never seen a married couple who didn't.

"And I'm his auntie!" Sammy said with a grin. "You guys did so good with this little guy."

Arch smiled, walking over to her and looking down at his son. "I still can't believe we made such a perfect baby," he said.

Tabby laughed. "The perfect half comes from me."

He shook his head. "You're a mess, Tabby O'Donnell."

"But I'm *your* mess now."

"You sure are."

Sammy took that as her cue to leave. "I'm going to run to the bakery and get some kolaches while I can. You guys need anything?"

Tabby shook her head. "Just those books. For now, I'm going back to bed. Little Wright has been keeping me up all night every night. Eventually he has to stop that."

Sammy nodded. "He will." She handed the baby to Arch as she got to her feet. "He's going to love his daddy."

Arch smiled and nodded. "I hope so."

Sammy let herself out, driving to the bakery. She got triple the number of kolaches she usually did and drove into town. She knew that Barry still hadn't tried them, and she wanted him to understand her love for kolaches.

When she got to the bookstore, she was surprised that the little parking lot was full. Surprised, but happy. She walked to the door and saw that Barry was sitting at the desk ringing up a couple of customers. There were more waiting for him.

Everyone in line was clutching multiple books. Sammy couldn't be more excited for him. She walked around the desk and sat in the chair beside him, setting the bag of kolaches on the counter. She had no idea how to ring people up, or she would have immediately started helping.

Instead as each person came to the front, she thanked them for coming and engaged in a bit of conversation. "How did you hear about the bookstore?"

"My sister just had a baby. She said her midwife married the man who owned the store the day of the birth, and she wanted everyone to be supportive of the store. I think she must have called thirty people at least. A group of us drove over from Haskell earlier today."

"I delivered the baby." Sammy grinned. "I'm Sammy Ross."

"No, you're not!" Barry protested. "You're Sammy Hamilton."

Sammy shrugged. "Newlywed. I forgot." She'd considered keeping her last name, but . . . he was very excited about it. She would have to take his last name after all.

"My sister said such amazing things about you," the woman told her. "Would you take a patient from Haskell?"

"Of course I would!" Sammy smiled. "You'd have to be able to drive to my clinic in time for the birth, though."

"It's not that far. I could do it." The girl grinned. "I'll get your information from my sister and make an appointment. I just found out I was pregnant a couple of weeks ago."

"Well, I'll look forward to seeing you, then."

Barry took the girl's money and bagged her books. "You're bringing me customers," he said softly. "I should have married you sooner."

Sammy laughed. "People just had to know you were here. That's the whole thing."

"Well, I guess they've figured it out." He checked out the last person in line and turned to her. "What did you bring me?"

"Kolaches. I think I told you about them. I got four different flavors for us to try."

He dug into the bag and pulled out one of the little treats. "It just looks like a hunk of dough."

"It's so much more than that!" She bit into hers and showed him the insides. "This one is sausage and cheese. I think it's my favorite except the bacon and cheese and the lemon-filled and the . . . Okay, I love them all!"

Barry bit into his kolache and stared at it for a moment. "This is good!"

Sammy nodded emphatically. "They make them fresh every morning. I want to move into the bakery just for the kolaches."

"I think I could live off these things." He looked into the bag to see how many there were. "So we each got six?"

Sammy laughed. "Four for me and eight for you."

"I think I love you, Sammy Hamilton."

Just as he said the words, the door opened to the store, and in came Karlan and Hope Culpepper. Hope hurried over to Sammy. "He's still not happy that it's a girl. He's going to fall in love with his little princess, though, isn't he?"

"Of course he will." Sammy grinned at Karlan. "I had nothing to do with the gender of your baby!"

Karlan wrinkled his nose. "Okay, where are the mysteries?"

Barry jumped up and showed Karlan to the books he was looking for. "What are you looking for?" Sammy asked Hope.

"Romance. Karlan keeps me happy, but every woman needs just a little more romance in her life, doesn't she?"

"I would think so." Sammy led Hope to the small romance section. "Barry is going to beef up this section based on my recommendations."

"Barry is a smart man."

Chapter 10

Sammy spent the day at the bookstore with Barry, helping out with everything she could. She learned to run the POS system and helped shelving books. As trade-ins, he'd gotten a lot of romances, and she worked on expanding the romance area.

By the time the store closed, she was tired. "What do you want for supper?" she asked as they headed out the door. She had a bag of books she would deliver to her sister the following day tucked under her arm.

"Do you want to do the diner? Or Bob's? Or we could even head to Laramie for a meal."

"I don't think I should go that far from the clinic. Not when I'm the only one on call. It hurts that Tabby is out. I'm sorry, but we're stuck here in town."

He shrugged. "Let's do the diner, if you're all right with that. I don't want to cook, and I don't think you do either."

Sammy grinned. "I *rarely* want to cook!"

"Then the diner it is." He led her to his truck. "We'll pick yours up after church tomorrow, if that's all right. If you need to go anywhere tonight, it'll just be the clinic, right?"

She nodded. "Right. And I don't have anyone else within two weeks of due date. We should be good. But just in case . . ."

"No, I can understand that. When Tabby is working again, I'm taking you to Laramie for some Thai food."

"Sounds good to me." She got into his truck with him and leaned back in the passenger seat. "We should grocery shop after we eat. The cupboards are getting bare."

He nodded. "I almost stopped one evening this week, but I wasn't sure what you usually buy, and I thought it would be better if I waited for you."

"Always better to wait for me. Mundane chores are better if we do them together."

Once they were sitting at the diner, he glanced down at the menu. "What's good here?"

She shrugged. "Not sure. I get the same thing every single time. I'm a creature of habit, you know."

"I have noticed that about you. I'm surprised you don't just plan for the same meal every night. Mondays you have soup. Tuesdays you have grilled cheese."

She tilted her head to one side. "You know . . . that would make things easier. Maybe not every week the same, but how about we make up a menu tomorrow? We can hang it on the fridge, and whoever is home from work first can start cooking?"

"Sounds good to me."

"Have you been writing in the evenings?"

He nodded. "Some. I got a little done early in the week, and then the last couple of nights after you've gone to bed. I figure if I can get this book ready, it might make me feel better if the bookstore crashes and burns."

"The bookstore seemed to be doing great today. Are you still worried about that?"

"A little, but not as much as I was. The word of mouth has been amazing."

After they'd both ordered, she looked over at him. He'd told her he loved her right before they were interrupted. She felt the same for him, but did she tell him that now? Or did she wait for a more appropriate time?

After a little deliberation, she decided to wait until they were home that evening. She wished she had more kolaches to give him as part of her declaration, but she'd think of something.

After dinner, they went to the grocery store, and each of them grabbed items willy nilly. It's how she liked to shop. When they were done, he frowned at their shopping cart. "I think a menu will help us not buy a million things from the store, too."

She shrugged. "Probably. Are you usually organized about shopping?"

He shook his head. "No, but I feel like I should be."

"Nah. It's more fun not to be." She grinned. "I love getting home and being all excited when I open the bags that I bought and not remembering half of it."

He laughed. "I'm not sure that's the right way to do things . . ."

"That's what I love about life. There's rarely one right or wrong way to do things. If you do them how it feels natural to you, then it's probably right for you."

"Interesting philosophy."

"I'll have to write a book about it someday," she said with a grin.

As they were unpacking the groceries, he realized she was right. He looked at some of the things that came out of the bags and couldn't help but wonder what they'd been thinking purchasing them. "Why did we buy Jell-O?"

"I bought lime Jell-O for a lemon cake. I try to always have that on hand in case there's a surprise wedding and I need to take a dish. Or a surprise anything. We have lots of pop up potlucks around here."

"What on earth is a pop up potluck?"

"Well, it's when someone calls and says, 'We have an event tomorrow. Everyone is bringing a dish.' If they don't tell me I can't bring dessert, then I take a lemon-lime cake."

"And if they say you can't bring a dessert?"

"I always keep a frozen shepherd's pie in the freezer in the garage. I defrost and bake. Then I have my potluck dish ready."

He grinned. "And you say you aren't organized!"

"Only about pop up potlucks. Nothing else in my life is half as organized."

"I have a hard time believing that."

She shrugged. "Believe what you will. I'm really not organized at all."

"I suppose . . ."

Sammy put the last thing into the fridge and walked into the living room. "Grocery shopping is done for the week. I think we should watch a movie."

"I like watching movies with you!"

She laughed. "No, I mean really watch a movie. We've never done that before!"

He frowned. "I can always think of parts of you I'd like to be touching during movies . . ."

"You're an absolute mess, Barry. I think that's why I love you so much."

He stared at her for a moment. "Really? You love me?"

"I wouldn't have married you if I wasn't already half in love with you. And then you were so wonderful about me being called away over and over this week. I guess that cemented it for me. I'm so glad we're married."

He wrapped his arms around her, resting his cheek on the top of her head. "I love you, too, Sammy."

She stayed like she was for a moment, just glorying in the feel of him and knowing he loved her. "I guess I knew what I was talking about when I walked into the bookstore announcing I loved you."

"Of course you did. I have a store named Barry's Books!"

"And soon, it will have lots more romances!"

He grinned, kissing her head. "It sure will. My sweet little Sammy is going to take care of that for me."

"You just show me where you order your books from, and I'll take care of it."

He sighed happily. "Everything seems to be going my way. I have a wife to love, I'll hopefully soon have a kid or two to love, and my brother is moving to town to work with me. I would say everything is coming up roses."

"You really do like that movie *Gypsy* don't you?"

"Yes, I really do." He smiled. "It was one of my mom's favorites, so I got to know it well."

"When am I going to meet her?" she asked.

He sighed. "I want to say never, but that's not fair. She has the right to know she has a new daughter-in-law. I'll call her and see what she says."

"That would be great!" She grinned at him. "I will introduce you to my parents eventually, too."

"You will?"

She nodded. "I guess I should call them and tell them I'm married. I was planning to Monday night, but everything got all crazy with deliveries."

"Do you think the full moon is why we got married?" he asked.

She laughed. "Absolutely not. I think we got married because we had feelings for each other . . . and because you couldn't keep it in your pants."

"I guess I should work on that, shouldn't I?"

"Everyone should . . ."

Epilogue

Ten months later, it was Sammy's turn to be on the delivery table. "You're doing great, Sam. Wright's going to have a cousin any minute now!" Tabby told her.

Barry was at her side, mopping the sweat off her forehead. "I'm glad you're here for this," she told him just as another contraction hit her.

Dallas stood ready to bathe the baby as soon as it emerged. "I'm so happy you invited me to be part of this!" She was very swollen with child as well, due in only a few weeks.

"Push, Sammy! You can do it!" Tabby said, her hands out and ready to catch the baby as it emerged.

Twenty minutes later, Barry and Sammy were left alone with their new daughter. "She's perfect!" Sammy said for the twentieth time. "No matter how many births I've been through, my little girl is the most beautiful baby on the whole planet."

Barry smiled. "I wasn't expecting her to be quite so gray . . ."

"It's the vernix. It'll be gone soon, and she'll be nice and pink and ready to take the world by storm."

"Just like her mama?"

"Absolutely." Sammy laid back on the bed, still cradling the baby against her. "Do you want to hold her?"

Barry had never really held a baby, but he nodded. "I'll try."

"Just be sure to support her head and hug her against you. You'll do just fine."

To his surprise, Sammy was right. Holding his little girl this way was the most wonderful thing he'd ever done. "Thank you for giving me such a beautiful little girl."

Sammy smiled, tears filling her eyes as she watched father with daughter. "I love you both so much."

Barry looked at her with awe. "I love you, too. I can't believe we grew this beautiful baby all on our own."

"She's a true child of love."

About the Author

www.kirstenandmorganna.com[1]

Also by Kirsten Osbourne

To sign up for Kirsten Osbourne's mailing list and receive notice of new titles as they are available, click here.[1]

Interested in more romances featuring Kirsten's signature brand of silliness? A complete list of her romances is available here[2].

---

1. http://eepurl.com/y6WRb

2. http://www.kirstenandmorganna.com/super-secret-link-page/